# PERRAS MALAS

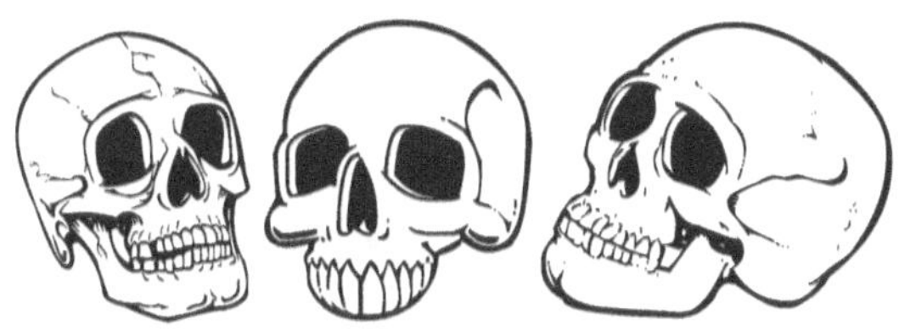

# MANNY TORRES

Outcast Press
Fiction From the Fringes

# DEDICATION

To my grandmother

& all the women who have survived abusive men and to the women who did not survive abusive men. To every woman who has survived toxic masculinity, misogyny, sexual assault and domestic violence:

These acts of vengeance are for you.


— Manny Torres

"What! Will these hands ne'er be clean?"


— Lady Macbeth

# INTERREGNO

Crows blotted out the sun. The gray sky was crowded with them. Diving and swooping, a maelstrom of flapping wings and angry caws.

Mariposa leaned out of the small sports car's passenger seat, looking back at Kika, cautious of the swirling cyclone of carrion birds. The sky was marked with them like strokes of charcoal on a cloud canvas. Her ears throbbed from its twisting, violent roar, sucking the wind from her lungs. Her heart was a jackhammer. Eyes felt as if they would explode. She looSked at what Kika was doing after she'd promised herself never to look again, then leaned over between her legs and vomited. Her face was hot, her ears crammed with the whirling din. But it wasn't the sky falling or twisting from above causing the din. It was her murderous partner dispersing with her black energy. The type of violent dynamism that could crack the earth open or bring the sky down on top of them.

Crows circled, waiting their turn at the dead man's eyes.

"What do we do with him?" Mari shouted.

The man sat in dirt thickened by blood, sitting against the perimeter fence of the landfill, his chin limply resting against his chest. No longer a face but a rearrangement of bone, torn skin, and gristle. Kika thought of leaving his eyes for the carrion-feeders. She loomed over him, tire iron in one hand, pliers in the other. Opera gloves of blood.

Hell hath no fury like a woman tornado.

"Let's fuck his corpse and then leave him to the crows," Kika laughed. "Sound good to you? The other frat boys won't even recognize him."

The ground shook.

Kika would have spit, but her mouth was dry. A collar of blood went up her neck, up to her chin. "I'm not sure if I still want to cut off his cock," Kika said. "He's not going to need it, and it might be an overstatement if I clipped it." She struck his head again with the rounded end of the tire iron to see if he was still dead. She tossed the pliers into the shrubbery. "Get the fuck out of the car, girl. It's not going anywhere."

Mari hesitated. Kika's tremendous eyes swelled with napalm, her mouth pinched to a thin slit. She approached Mari like she was going to walk through her. In the short time they'd known each other, things had gotten way out of hand.

"Should we tie him up?" Mari asked.

Kika ignored her, standing in the middle of the road. Looking up at the sky as if calling the crows to action. "Strip him."

"Where's the tape?" asked Mari.

"Use a tampon string, stupid." Kika threw the crowbar at her. "He's fucking dead. Leave him naked for the crows to finish." Kika's gaze followed Mari from where she stood, slowly grinning. Hair caked against her shoulders, black dress loose and frayed at the hem. Black half-moons beneath her eyes. Kika appeared as if she could shape-shift into an entire flock of birds, transform to a phoenix and torch the entire city in a single sweep.

When Mari kneeled beside the man, he was a dead lump. She tried not to look at the ratatouille of his face or lumpy brain mass exposed through a hole in his scalp. No teeth. Bottom of his mouth torn and dangling. Fingers missing. Legs broken and twisted unnaturally. Stray dogs would finish him off.

Mari looked at her own hands. The raw knuckles. She vomited again after stripping his pants to his ankles. She tore off the remains of his shirt. He had shit himself and it smeared her hands.

"It's just shit." Kika looked over her shoulder. "Don't be scared. We're all shit."

# 1.

# MI HERMANA, LA PERRA

# CH. ONE

They were into body sculpting and hair gel. Pointed shoes and high collars. Gold chains on sweaty chests, diamond earrings. Except for the fat guy driving. He looked like an albino bulldog wearing a sideways baseball cap.

It was 3:47AM and the car rolled out of the club parking lot, cruising the next few blocks. Red lights were suggestions. They stopped, heading west. There was laughter and shouting. The back door opened and the girl with the blue wig and furry, pink purse fell out, landing on her hands, then falling to her side.

The two in the backseat cheered her disaster.

The driver yelled, "We promise not to show the video to your mom!"

"Fuck you," she casually spat because this was routine. Her black eyeliner melted, knees bled. Back tires spun close to her face.

They made the intersection and were gone. Back to cruising.

"Bro, I'm spent," Omar said at the wheel.

"Take us back to the diner, O," Mr. Sensation said from the back. His bronze tan glowed with sick radiation. It was a glow you could smell. "Then drop me off at home. You can sleep all you want tomorrow, all right, homie?"

"How'd I wind up chauffer tonight?" Omar said.

"You always the chauffeur, bro." Hassle cackled.

"Fuck that, bro," Omar said. "Hey, hey. Listen. My girl is waiting for me back home."

They booed and threw empty beer cans at him.

"Wait, wait, stop," Omar shouted. "Hey, look at that." Omar's finger followed a woman they drove up on, walking parallel to the car on the sidewalk. "It's that bitch again."

"It ain't." Sensation sat up, suddenly sober. "'Cause how'd that hoe get up here so fast? We left her ass back on the other street. She didn't just jog here. Not in the shape we left her."

"It's her," Omar said.

"What, she suddenly changed into a new dress? That ain't her, man. This hoe is different. Ain't never seen her before. She one of Blitz's new girls?"

"Blitz don't pimp that much no more," Omar said.

"Fuck it," Hassle said. "Let's pick her up."

"Gimme some cash, bro."

Omar dropped something into Mr. Sensation's hand and he handed it to Hassle, who stuck a sweaty wad of money out the passenger window.

The woman looked like nightclub leftovers, staggering crookedly, very disheveled. The car honked several times before she stopped. She stood perfectly still, shading her eyes against the high-beams. Her sunglasses reflected the bright light, making her eyes incendiary. She had a narrow face, like a starved fennec. Lipstick was smudged, not smeared. Her straight, black hair fell below her shoulders. Long, black dress to her ankles, ragged and muddy around the hem. She carried an antique suitcase.

"Crazy witch," Omar said.

Turning and facing them, she approached the passenger side. Taking her time. Black boots stepping quietly. She leaned into the window, one hand on the door, fingers drumming. They were long fingers with nails ripped to the quick. Manly hands, smudged with motor oil, her knuckles bruised and cut. She removed her sunglasses. There were scrapes and fresh scratches on her chin and cheek, a fading black eye, along with a necklace of black and blue marks around her throat.

"*¿Hablas español?*" Omar heckled.

"Damn, you raggedy, bitch," Hassle said. "What the fuck happened to you?"

Face obscured, she murmured, "A little late to the party, aren't you boys?"

"We the after-party, baby," Mr. Sensation said from the backseat. "Where you going? Get in. We all about having a good time."

She couldn't make out his face but he held tiny liquor bottles between each finger.

"Nice, you brung plenty for everybody," Sensation said. "After we do this, we'll get some pancakes."

"Well then." She could barely maintain her smile. "Let me come on board."

Omar said, "How about we come on you? Ha-ha!"

"You think you got enough juice for that, little boy?" she said.

"Yo, man," Hassle said. "Shut the fuck up, O. That's no way to treat a lady. Get in, baby. You can sit on my lap."

"For the three of you is $30 each," she advised.

"$30?" Omar said. "The fuck you gonna do for $30? We best get the whole works for that much."

"$30 each just for the ride along. Anything else is negotiable along the way."

# CH. TWO

The sky over the town always looked on the brink of rain.

"How far are we taking it?" Reynolds had asked Detective Funzo over the phone as he navigated a garbage sea. Spread out to the east side of Carbon, Georgia, the landfill occupied the unfinished excavation for the stadium promised to many broken-hearted taxpayers. The massive crater was now filled and covered over with mounds of trash high enough to be seen from the highway. Toward the west were half-built, uninhabited condos and an abandoned hospital. Beyond that was the bay that opened to the Atlantic. The air was briny, weighing heavily on the lungs and eyes, inducing headaches.

"How far are we going with this?" Reynolds asked.

"End of the line. It stops here," Detective Funzo responded. "That's as far as we can take it. There's plenty more room once we get those bulldozers."

"I don't mean that," Reynolds said.

The detective surveyed the landfill from inside his car. "Yeah, well, we went too far this time. I get it. We destroyed something that should have been left alone. What was Phil thinking? You can't trust any of those whores and their deathtrap pussies."

"It's the only thing left to enjoy these days," Reynolds said.

"I heard he kept one and took one for later," said Funzo. "Where'd he take her?"

"He didn't want me touching her. Stupid bitch got what she deserved. Took her back to the West End Motel."

"Well, it's cleaner than the one on the east end." Detective Funzo chuckled.

"Somewhere that he can do his thing," said Reynolds.

"Jesus, you see the fog this morning? How?"

"It's moisture, suspended in the air."

"I know where fog comes from," Funzo said. "I'm not stupid."

"Ground's kind of warm right now," Reynolds said. He slowed the car. "You sure they were all dead when they were interred?"

"The fuck you mean? Of course, they were dead. I didn't kill them, I just supervised the burial. We got a few more to finish. Work's never done. Christ."

"I can't breathe in this," Reynolds said. "Air's kind of wet and cold. Mix those two and there's your fog."

"What is this, science class?" Funzo said. "Are you out here? No, you're at home in your air-conditioned living room. Who the fuck cares? You didn't seem phased when the Albanians dumped their corpses. You were cold and precise. How it should be. That's what I'm trying to instill in these spic motherfuckers we got in the crew."

"Should I have been fazed? It's not like the lawyer can do any of this cleanup shit. You know, do all the dirty work? I was there yesterday so don't give me no shit."

# CH. THREE

That one time, not long ago, before the fires, Eastern Europeans had visited Carbon, Georgia. No place like it in the USA. Moldovans, Albanians, Russians, Ukrainians—didn't matter. To Carbonites, they were the same. They all looked the same, at least. They had the same accent, same smell, and looked like they'd been sleeping in their clothes since 1986. Clothes that looked like Americans threw them out decades ago. They were a skinny flock, so pale they looked yellow. And mustaches. Waxy handlebars dripping over their pointed chins. They'd shown up in an old, brown Cadillac hearse as like to impress them. Real gaudy, four of them riding in like kings, wearing old polyester church suits that smelled like a moldy mattress. Ugly, swampy teeth, stinky beards. Greasy pompadours and strange, pointed boots.

Blitz made a face that was somewhere between a grin and squint. At least they wore suits to the meeting.

The man behind the wheel of the hearse had introduced them.

"These mens, they like to party, my friend." His accent was comical, like a comedian who'd never actually spoken to or known an Eastern European trying to affect their speech pattern. The kind of accent you'd hear on some short-lived TV sitcom. Soon they were at the gate, entering the expansive landfill, rolling over a sea of trash. Garbage hills to the north, behind which stood rows of public housing cubes. To the south was a maze of crushed cars. Driving eastward would take you directly to Carcass Bay and the ocean.

Sitting on a garbage dune was a rusted bulldozer half-sunk into the compost. The backhoe loader next to it fared better, at least it seemed to have a future here in the landfill after repairs were completed. The machine sat abandoned, side hatch opened, exposing its sick engine. Surrounding it were scrap parts and a half-dozen jerry cans. And random garbage.

"We call this the Humps," Blitz had told the Eastern European driver.

"Da Humps? Ha ha ha," the driver had said. His name was Casimir, but Blitz had forgotten it already. "Because it looks like hump over the land. I gettit, I gettit!"

Reynolds was there to oversee the overseeing of the work crew. Third in command and dressed like a dad from a 1970's TV comedy: cheap beige and brown suit. Black, shellacked hair, neatly slicked back. Irvine Park brown loafers. With him was Blanco, the balding ex-boxer with a speech impediment.

Phil was Blitz's older brother, but they looked nothing alike. Phil had feathered, blow-dried hair all in place, handlebar pornstache like a has-been Marlboro Man. Shirt collar popped around his neck. He had the coke bloats, puffy bags under his eyes. He stood firm as timber with a hangover crackling across his eyes and forehead. Sleeves rolled up like he was going to do some digging when it was always Blanco and the other boys who did the dirty work. He took out a handkerchief and inhaled the cheap cologne poured into it. The cheap-suit mafia didn't seem affected by the stink of the landfill.

Phil waved at the men and they waved back.

"Make it quick," Phil had said to Funzo while leaning on Reynolds. "This place stinks."

"You expecting the aroma of petunias?" Funzo said. The detective was a thickset slob in a trench coat streaked with coffee stains. Rumpled salt and pepper hair greased back, tie pulled down and disregarded.

"Who's working on the backhoe?" Reynolds asked.

Phil shrugged. "Is it broken? Maybe we can get Barry to look at it. He does mechanic work."

"On airplanes," Reynolds said.

"Stop worrying so much about the details," Phil said.

"I mean, we dropped a few grand on that thing, we should expect it to work. And who left those gas cans there? Meth heads love stealing that shit. Thing's not even moving."

"Until we install the gas line," Phil said. "I'm going to have the boys haul those in for refueling."

"Gas line?" Reynolds said. "Are you kidding? You finally strike up a deal with the Texan to lay down a pipeline?"

"Yeah, we're just talking right now. Relax, man. Shit is building up so fast, it's wont to make your head spin. Building this business is like raising the fucking Titanic. But I've put my fingers in every pie I can. You worry about getting the boys all lined up, and Seth and me will take care of everything else. I have in mind to eventually install some gas tanks right where you're standing. When we get our fleet of garbage trucks, they'll be able to refuel here."

"That's really fucking ambitious."

"Baby steps." Phil rubbed his forehead and closed his eyes. "Goddamn it. Right here. It fucking hurts right here."

From this distance, Reynolds watched Blitz and Funzo talk. Casimir walked them to the hearse and showed them the contents in the back. Blitz and some of his crew helped Blanco carry several stiff corpses out to the trench they'd dug.

"This is all just a formality," Phil said. "They could have thrown those into Carcass Bay and been done with it."

"Their toxic waste is next," Reynolds said.

"That's part of the deal." Phil shaded his face. The ache crawling over his head felt like shifting tectonic plates.

"Did you forget, we live here and breathe these fumes, Phil?" Reynolds shook his head.

"By the time that happens, they'll have invented dome cities we can live in and we'll have all the fresh, clean air pumped in from underground oxygen tanks."

"That makes no sense, but okay. I'm sure I'll be retiring to New Mexico by then."

"It's just trash, man," Phil said.

"You can say that 'cause you live in White Oak. What happens when they haul in the radioactive shit?"

Phil shrugged.

"You gonna oversee the burial?" Reynolds asked.

Phil shrugged and shook his head.

"Heh," Reynolds said. "You been hanging around Seth a lot. Afraid to get your hands dirty too?"

"He set this up," Phil said. "Once in a while, I have to go into the trenches to supervise. We wouldn't normally be out here, but this is the pitch meeting. I had to be here. Eventually, you're going to handle all this shit. On your own."

Reynolds surveyed the sea of garbage. Seagulls and crows fought for supremacy. The crows always came out ahead. He said, "Any responses from Palermo and his contract? I mean, Carbon has one garbage truck for the whole fucking city. Always looks like there's a garbage man strike. We're going to need at least six more trucks, and at least four bulldozers. We need machines that actually work."

"That's on the list of things Seth is handling," Phil said. "Don't worry about it."

"Yeah, but in the meantime, you're using my men to dig these holes."

"Who told them to be such good ditch-diggers? These Spanish boys came to this country for a better life and we're offering it to them. Have faith in what we're making here, man."

Reynolds watched them work. "They're not even putting down lye. One or two corpses is one thing, but you can't just raw dog a mass grave like that. You gotta sprinkle something before throwing them in, then frost them before they bury it."

When they completed the burials, Blitz, his crew, and Funzo laughed with Casimir and the group in the hearse while Phil and Reynolds stood by watching.

"Carbon's gonna be the water around the garbage island," Reynolds said.

"We're not a beach town, man," Phil said.

"Where are the guns?"

Phil cocked his head at the crew. Blitz, Blanco, and Funzo began pulling wooden crates from the back of the hearse. Among their ranks was Embra. She backed a small trailer at a 45-degree angle from the hearse and supervised the loading.

"She's holding on to them until the trade," Phil said.

Funzo moved and pointed like a traffic cop, explaining to their guests that they'd eventually get the machinery to bury and flatten whatever they had to dispose of. Blitz and Embra took inventory of the crates' contents.

"That's all Cold War surplus shit," Reynolds said. "From Croatia or wherever-the-fuck."

"Our buyers don't know that shit," Phil said. "They just want grease guns and cartridges, so we're going to deliver the order."

"They better fucking work."

"You know what the market price is for medical waste recovery?"

"I don't," said Reynolds. "Did you ever consider that when their trash piles high enough and wide enough, they might try to claim it as their territory? Mark my words, it can happen."

Phil looked at him with one eye closed.

"Trash is trash," Phil said. "The idea is to bring revenue from any and all sources, right? One day this will all be condos and shopping malls."

Reynolds looked to the south, where a complex of condos lined the downtown strip. "That's what they said when they poured concrete for the hospital and the strip," he said. "That's what they promised when they dug up the stadium." He pulled a cigarette from inside his jacket and stuck it in his mouth but didn't light it.

"Sounds like you've been talking to the detective, letting all his crazy conspiracies fog your common sense," Phil said.

"He's not wrong," said Reynolds.

"But he's nuts. You're not usually a complainer. You're a problem solver. You'll get it. And don't worry about what we bury. Think of it as job security."

"I didn't sign up to be a garbage man. Are they spending the night in Carbon?"

"Our guests always stay in our fine province," Phil said. "I'm going over there to seal the deal."

"They went through their women," Reynolds said. "Now they'll fuck with our girls."

"So?" Phil said. "That's why they're there."

"Our tracks are thinning out. And these motherfuckers are stingy as fuck. They're lousy tippers. Our girls hate them."

Phil left to shake hands with the Eastern Europeans.

Reynolds signaled Blanco to come over to him. "Hey, listen," Reynolds told him. "If they stay at the hotel, burn the sheets when they leave. In fact, burn everything. Pillows, towels, the fucking plates they eat off."

"Right, boss," Blanco said. "Bedbugs."

# CH. FOUR

The building was more of a cube than a monolith, the newest building in Carbon, as if transported from a clean, futuristic place. A hexahedron of chrome, glass, and steel sitting on a cul-de-sac overlooking Carcass Bay. Vacant offices and suites. Towering above the garbage heaps, the humps that could be seen from almost anywhere in town. An effort to erase the scab of a cursed town, rebuild it into the 21st century, make it look like a real city.

"Big time." Barrel-chested Reynolds could feign almost anything. In this business, he did. He had big fists and a logical mind, but the shit-eating grin was his superpower.

Seth peeled back the decal that left the words **Seth Nelstrum, Esq.** across the glass door.

"This some classy furniture you got here," Reynolds said.

"Like it, huh? From Sweden," Seth said. He was a pallid, freckled adherent in his baggy, gray suit and maroon wool tie. He wore brown, clunky shoes that looked like loaves of bread. "That's where the big table's going. Like the *Last Supper*. That's where all the business will happen. Take it off the street, give it a corporate makeover. We'll sit it out, Phil at the head. Put out some muffins and orange juice. Have weekly meetings. Plot. Have some serious talks. Put the business where it needs to be. Isolated from everything, other groups, families, investigators. A dream situation come true."

"Who delivered all this shit up here?"

"Sensation and his boys rolled it all up here." Seth polished the lettering. He was long and slim, with short, blond hair. Ginger, really. Ginger eyebrows, even the hair on his knuckles.

"All the way up here? How about that. Did Blitz help too?"

"You kidding?" Seth chuckled. "That stoned motherfucker couldn't lift his own ass off the couch."

Reynolds leaned on the new leather seat, hands tucked in his pockets. "You throw something extra at them?"

"Nah. What for?"

"*What for* is you took them off a job that I had to finish while they were here moving shit. And you'd be surprised what Blitz is capable of doing if you ask him."

"All in a day's work," Seth said. "Who gives a fuck? They work for us. Doesn't matter if they're out there burying 'treasures' all day or cleaning out the whorehouse. They're supposed to do what we tell them."

"Yeah, but not this shit." Reynolds poked a finger in his palm. "Not unless you're paying them extra. They're not on your payroll."

"Says who?" Seth stopped and looked at him from the door. "Phil said it was okay."

"Says me, man. That's my payroll."

"Phil did say it was okay. Bitch at him."

"You went over my head. I'm still the pit boss. Phil's a CEO but I'm the one barking out orders. You're just the legal guy. Remember that. Let's keep the rank and structure the way it's supposed to be."

"It's one of the perks, man," Seth said.

"Nah, fuck all that. I'm trying to keep those motherfuckers in line. This kind of shit undermines my level of command."

"Whatever, man."

"Whatever? Fuck you. Do your part and I'll do mine. Just remember that."

"Hey, man," Seth said. "All right. Relax. It's just this one time. Next time, I'll clear it with you. And tip them good. And guess what else is coming to Carbon?"

"What's that?"

"The Chinese."

Reynolds nodded slowly as if he understood. "How's that?"

"We're cutting some deals via the Albanians. Chinese burials. When we get our fleet of trucks, we'll be able to accommodate Chinese burials."

"What the fuck is a Chinese burial?"

"They cremate their dead over there. Some people have been promised a burial, but they're all out of room in the mainland. There are like seven billion Chinese people over there. We're offering them real estate for their dead. They've prepaid before dying. The money is in."

"They're bringing Chinese corpses way-the-fuck over here to be buried in the landfill?"

"That's the plan," Seth said. "Imagine… Plus, we'll be expanding territory to add additional landfills."

"Yeah, the fucking ground will be saturated in soy sauce real soon," Reynolds said.

"We're setting that up for a five-year plan. It's lucrative. So, tell me. What's going on with you? A little hostile there over some furniture. Bad night at the club?"

"Nah. Fuck it. That kid Billy is way past his payday."

"I was afraid of that. Time he catches those hands, am I right?"

"Worse than that. Phil is... Let me explain. These boys get soft sometimes. They watch those stupid gangster movies and think they're rock stars 'cause they have guns and sell coke, and have a stable of women. Then they think they're a cartel if they successfully close a single deal. Then come the groupies, hangers-on. People start coming in from everywhere, latching on. Money and product hemorrhages. Then there's Billy... You know where this is going? We gotta have a talk with him."

"So, you're in for a busy week?"

"Yeah." Reynolds crossed his arms. "Big party."

# CH. FIVE

There used to be a Woolworths supermarket on the strip a decade or so ago. Used to be the center of commerce when the town was a stopover between Jacksonville and Savannah. You couldn't recognize it now, but for the arabesque trimming and the faux columns out front. Now it was painted over, black and purple with flashy green letters across the front. Cigarette butts and flyers littered the sidewalk. The strip was mostly bars and nightclubs, though half the businesses were shuttered. On this strip was also a wig store, and several eateries. A church and a rehab center.

There was a darkness to the street as if a black hole was slowly consuming it. Streetlamps buzzed like dying fireflies.

The street was barren. She'd come in with the wind, carrying a small suitcase, walking up two blocks past the club. She crossed an empty lot to a big, sky-blue 24-hour corner store and gas station. Outside was a mural of several dead hip-hop artists.

In her damaged dress, she floated, X-ray eyes behind Eurotrash sunglasses. She took money out of her bra and paid for cigarettes at the store. The money was greasy with spray tan, hair gel, and pussy juice. Money she'd taken from the three boys in the car.

The motions of murder came easily now, how she flitted in a miasma of violence. Quick and precise. They hadn't expected it. She didn't see them coming but it was a mutual end. It had gotten messy.

"Do I need a key for the bathroom?" she asked the clerk, a tan man of unknown origin, hiding behind a big, black mustache.

Being a man who minded his business, he momentarily stared at his reflection in her sunglasses. His gaze broke. He'd grown tired of looking at himself, focusing instead on this degenerate prom queen in ragged leather heels, the broken straps dragging around her ankles. Her feet were greasy, bloody.

He handed her a wooden paddle with a key chained to the end. He pointed outside and around the corner, curiously looking at the suitcase she dragged with her.

The bathroom mirror was smudged with human filth. She pissed, washed her hands. The dispenser sprinkled gray powdered soap on her hands. Most of the blood washed off. She returned the key and browsed the beer cooler, humming to herself before grabbing the biggest bottle of malt liquor. The clerk wiped his hands on his pants after she told him to keep the change. She strutted outside with the large bottle of brown liquid, tore the cap, and took a gulp. She immediately puked it all out, so poured the rest of the drink over the patch of her vomit. She sat on a trashcan for some time, willing the sun to stay asleep, having no idea what time it was. She brushed herself off. The dress probably had another day left before it would disintegrate.

She walked back inside and slapped a twenty-dollar bill on the counter.

"Pump number two, my good man." She drunkenly winked. But she wasn't drunk.

"Where's your car?" the man behind the mustache asked.

Outside, she rested her suitcase against a lamp post and went to the pump.

# CH. SIX

She retraced her steps as winds from Carcass Bay swept the dormant avenue. With one hand, she traced the name etched into the glass pane adorning a corner club. She remembered when this used to be Woolworths. She stood in the middle of the street, looked up, and spoke to the big, empty sky: "If You really existed, I'd ask for an apology. I think You owe a lot of people an apology. Things would be level after that. But You let them keep fucking up, on Your behalf. I know You gave up long ago, and You've been trying to clean up this mess for a long time. I'm here to help You to clean it up…"

She tore a long strip from her ragged seam and plugged the gas-filled malt liquor bottle. With the lighter she'd taken from one of the hair-gel boys, she lit then tossed it into the dark bar. There was a *boom* and, suddenly, the wood interior with its many stools, liquor bottles, and glasses ignited.

With pleasure, she watched the fire consume.

There was a wide, satanic grin staring back at her in the jagged glass. She let the flames tickle her face. She turned her back to the fire and walked off as it flickered against her back. By the time she reached the corner, the block grew with demonic incandescence. She crossed. Walked toward the overpass, where she'd parked the gel-boy's car. Real easy. She was on a roll. Still bleeding, still poking their boners at her, she'd left the mound of them in the backseat. She walked casually from the strip as two fire trucks drove past.

It'd been 36 hours since she'd slept. 48 since her stomach had been pumped. She circled the metro area several times, walked along the edge of Carcass Bay as the sun came up. The fire had been dowsed, a few cops and firemen stood around chatting from what she saw. She walked into a corner diner in a small shopping plaza and found a booth. The place hadn't been refurbished since 1973. She ate three fried eggs with hash browns, sausages, and a stack of pancakes. When she walked back outside, she threw up most of it on the sidewalk. Then she walked.

The morning sky was sapphire. The motel window allowed a view of the city: a smoky grid of orange and yellow dots in the fading murk of dawn.

Snowfall, inside her motel room.

On closer inspection, the small print of Gideon's Bible pages shredded to a million pieces.

Her prayer: "Oh, my Lord, why did You forsake us?"

The god of echoes did not respond.

"You deny us access to what is beyond the smokescreen. The ability to shatter all illusion."

Though she destroyed the inside of the bible, she kept it as a memento. Carved it out so she may crawl inside and sleep.

She showered and sat on the bed, wearing a robe and towel turban around her long, black hair. For a long time, she stared inside her open suitcase sitting on the other bed. There was a photo inside the netting of two young, unsmiling sisters in their school uniforms. There were two other photos behind it. Creased and faded remains of what she could salvage. She didn't have to hold them or look at them ever again. The newest one, the last they'd posed for, showed her sister breaking their solemn mood, tilting her head and winking, sticking out her tongue.

The images were forever imprinted in her memory, neither good nor sad. Just proof that they existed in that period of their lives.

Kika stared at the room phone for hours. It wasn't going to jump into her hands. She picked it up and dialed.

# CH. SEVEN

The neighborhoods in Carbon were a series of shotgun houses, cinderblock homes, and rows of mostly empty condos surrounding a landfill that could be seen from space. The downtown square, plaza, and strip were designed like a cardboard facsimile of New Orleans. The next great city that'd been abandoned.

Mari, hugging herself for warmth, crossed the toxic red desert of the landfill. Mari amidst the trash dunes. After all these years, she'd finally warmed to the stench. There was a street urchin pushing a shopping cart, ignoring her, deep in conversation with himself. A chipped statue of Jesus raised both arms from the junk collection in his cart. Blank stone eyes followed her.

The phone in her back pocket rang and just maybe it would be her calling.

"Jubilee?" Mari answered. She held the phone in both hands like she was caressing her girlfriend's face.

The woman calling echoed the name.

"Hello?" Mari said. "Who is this?" Her face froze with concern.

The woman's raspy voice seemed a million miles away. "Where's my sister?" she said.

"Who the fuck is this?" Mari hyperventilated.

"I need to tell my sister that I'm here for her. Put her on the phone."

"Jubilee's sister is dead! Don't try to fucking trick me! Who is this? I killed you!"

"Can't nobody kill me." The woman relaxed her whisper. "Can you just tell me where she is?"

"I have no fucking idea where she is!" Mari sobbed. "Are you a friend of Billy? 'Cause Billy's… gone. Billy is fucking dead."

"I don't know Billy." The woman was cold, distant. Practically a robot. "Tell me where Jubilee is."

"I have no fucking clue. Don't you get it?"

"Then tell me who the fuck are you and why do you have my sister's phone?"

"This is… Mari. Jubilee… was my girlfriend."

"What the fuck happened to her?"

"I don't know."

"You know."

"Long fucking story."

"You're going to tell me."

"This phone is dying," Mari said.

A short pause.

"Is the Latin Quarter still open?" the woman said.

"The one at the head of the strip? Yeah. But I can't be out in the open too long."

"Then tell me where and when. We'll meet there."

# CH. EIGHT

Three days ago, just outside Carbon, in that suburb of quiet streets and tidy lawns known as White Oak, Phil brought Barry to the townhouse for the weekend as a guest of honor. Every Barry visit was an excuse for debauchery, a grand BBQ party that could be smelled and heard across most of White Oak. Right there, among the vacant homes recently built on a figure-eight, isolated from everything, everywhere, and everyone. The white, two-story home stood surrounded by a wooden fence. Dogs ran around, catching Frisbees. The Jacuzzi boiled. The pool water clear and placid.

Lucky for everybody, the Eastern Europeans were long gone and back in South Florida.

Reynolds worked the grill. He was a hulk of a man with long, feathered hair straight out of 1978. His brow was thick, jutting over his face like some stone-chiseled blockhead from Marvel Comics. Wearing a collared shirt and slacks but still looking like a boss.

The labor pool of henchmen stood around, drinking beers and munching on trays of snacks laid out on two long tables. Salvadorians, Florida crackers, Dominicans, Mexicans, Puerto Ricans speaking in all their varied dialects. Knock-around guys standing around, waiting for work. Men who had since moved away or died. Mostly died.

"Joshua Milton. General in Liberia," Barry said with a twang that was halfway between South Carolina and Tennessee. "The Butt Naked General. True story." Barry had plenty of them. Once he showed up, all other conversations stopped, and a cluster gathered around him. They'd been standing around for hours and, finally, the steaks and chicken got slapped on the grill. The sun settled nicely over Carbon's smog cushion. Looked like a nuclear meltdown in limbo. The string lights kicked in, twinkling above their heads.

Barry was stocky, furry all over except his face. Bald but with a hair halo like Friar Tuck. His chest rug looked like a wool sweater exploding out of his shirt. Blitz stood near him, fading out the conversation, mesmerized by the reflection on his head. Amazed at his body hair yet concerned for the bald spot. Blitz was far enough away to seem interested but the look on his face marked him absent.

The henchmen, hangers-on, strippers, and call-girls tightened around Barry. Most of the girls were from Phil's club, or girlfriends and wives. Barry's muse and secretary, Katrina, a black girl with a joint always dangling from her mouth, never smiled at anyone. Always on guard beside him, watching everyone and everything. She kept a dagger strapped to one of her legs, even when she was wearing a bathing suit.

Phil, in *Miami Vice* regalia twenty years too late, laid next to Barry in his lounge chair, drinking beer from a plastic, gold-sparkled chalice. Thin dirtstache over his pouty lips, soft eyes with long lashes, like some greasy teen idol. He'd make a pretty girl if he was a cross-dresser or if he ever went to jail.

"Those niggers got liberated," Barry said. "But couldn't do nothing else but copy their former masters. Their village wars included young boys inducted with swords and AK-47s. Not surprisingly, they took after the colonialists. Monkey see, monkey do."

Blitz waited for a pocket of silence. "So, who's the Butt Naked General?"

Barry looked up at him through sunglasses. "General of the army in Liberia. He's a preacher now, but believed he could go straight into battle butt-naked and be invisible to his enemies. It must have worked if he made it out to see the Light of the Lord."

Everybody laughed.

"Goddamn," Blitz said.

"Yeah. Primitive superstitions." Barry was a world-trekking ex-con. A pilot. An importer of powdered product from the Caribbean and sometimes South America. "So, he'd go straight into battle wearing only boots, sword, and carrying his rifle. His long, black ding-aling flapping and flopping like a banana leaf!"

They laughed harder.

"And a big, white fucking smile." Phil toasted to the laughter before finishing off what was in his chalice. A girl in a bikini came by to refill it.

Music piped in from hidden speakers. Somewhere inside the house was Gums, the club DJ who worked for Blitz. Lots of Spanish music, sometimes country. A few girls danced under the canopy Reynolds had pitched next to the patio. Miguelito, the skinny boxer, stood on the other side of the giant grill, talking to his girlfriend, Neesy. She towered him. In her maroon velour dress, she looked like a Paleolithic Venus. She was a pale, freckled earth goddess with bright green eyes and lips like apple slices. Fake eyelashes and brown extensions that cascaded her shoulders. She nodded at everything Miguelito said, even though she'd heard it all before.

Barry watched the girls for a while, then turned to Phil. "Sex with her is like trying to fuck a couch, I imagine."

Phil giggled.

"Where's Chelmo?" Barry asked. "Your ranks thinning out or is it my imagination?"

Phil didn't say.

Barry said, "Boy, what a bullshitter Chelmo was. But he could dicker and wager like my old grandpappy. Geez. He must've had Jew blood in him."

"Chelmo hung himself," Blitz ceased the op to slip in.

"Goddamn," said Barry. When he spoke, they practically pressed their ears against him. "And Little Lutz with his ulcer. He died the same day they diagnosed it."

"Geez," Phil said. "They just couldn't handle the trade. I told them early on how it would go. They had fair warning. Have some guys do a quick stickup across town at some card game and one commits suicide, and the other one dies from internal bleeding from all his nervousness."

"Shit," said Barry. "You gettin' these boys straight out the locker room at Carbon High? You got some mean motherfuckers here, don't you?"

The chicken was done, so they passed around plates. Steaks were still cooking. Later, they ate stacks of pork shredded from the pig they'd roasted in a drum of coal and wood. There was more food than men and it kept piling up on the table. Miguelito's girl, Neesy, always had meat in her hands, surrounded by flirting men. Miguelito stood back, fuming, his arms crossed.

Blitz had taken some pills and drooled, leaving a trail of food from his softened paper plate. One of his groupies, a pale girl with a saggy face, who earlier had shown off tattoos of her favorite serial killers, was talking on the phone by a withered flowerbed. She was apologizing to her mother for all the drugs she'd just ingested and told her she would be home in a week. Blitz walked past her, and she was glowing neon green, with a cloaked figure no one else saw, floating over her. Someone had laced his joint with formaldehyde. Shermed him. His crew helped to keep him from falling over. Blanco went around, picking up the food he dropped. When no one was looking, he'd fist the leftovers into his mouth.

"Vega ran off with some crazy chick," Phil joked. "He hasn't been heard from. You taking inventory on my crews, Barry? Planning some kind of hostile takeover?"

Barry smiled uneasily and it seemed to deflate the vibes in his corner.

"Where's Billy?" Phil asked.

Most of the crew looked at each other. Reynolds came over, balancing a plate heavy with pork and potato salad on his beer can. He leaned close and whispered, "We're looking for him."

Phil shook his head.

"He hasn't returned my calls," said Reynolds.

"Or money. Or product. Did you get his last deposit?"

"If he made it, I don't know about it 'cause he sure didn't pay me a fucking cent."

Phil nodded, feigning a good time to jolly Barry. He waited for Barry to get distracted by some of the men before pulling Reynolds aside.

"You want Blitz in on this?" Reynolds asked. He finished most of his plate and handed it off to one of the passing girls. He placed his ear closer to Phil's mouth, the music was so loud.

"That asshole's completely useless now," Phil said.

"He's your brother, not mine," said Reynolds.

They alternated leaning into each other's ears.

"I saw him pop a few just now," Reynolds said. "Plus, he's been drinking all day. More fucked-up than usual. I'm not sure why. That boy's got anxiety."

"No. He's just an asshole," Phil said. "He gets the smaller cut anyway. I pay you more... But look, so Embra's holding the crates. Jamaicans are coming through."

"Coming here? To Carbon?"

"Yeah, they'll be here this week," Phil said. "Small family out of New Orleans. I'll be doing favors across the board for this, but the payoff's gonna be a stocking stuffer. Embra unloads, Barry gets a down payment, Jamaicans get what they want. Win-win."

"What are they doing with those guns?" Reynolds asked. "We're shit out of luck if they arm up against us. They'd just as soon take the town over, soon as you sell them that shit."

"That's the beauty of it, man. Nobody wants to take over Carbon. Who are you kidding?" Phil laughed. "Right now, it's a delicate situation. When the shit falls into place, it'll all start to make sense. Trust me, buddy."

Reynolds gave him an uncertain look. He hated being called buddy.

BBQ smokiness, dancing, more music. An impromptu boxing match started under the tent and twinkling lights. Abner and Miguelito went a few soft rounds before it devolved into a slap-match. Barry roared and cheered, clapping his big, hairy arms, not having seen this kind of action since prison.

Phil smiled encouragingly but went on talking with Reynolds. "We're going to look like jackasses if we don't make this deposit. He's going to think we're wasting his time. And we only get one chance with Barry. He's all smiles now 'cause there's pussy, beer, and shredded pork going around. But this honeymoon will end on Friday if we don't get this money in his hands."

"He puts on a good spread," Reynolds said.

"So does your wife, Rey." Phil snorted a bump out of his vial. "Seriously though, fuck him. I paid for all this shit. This is out of my pocket."

"Booze and schmooze, man."

"It was Seth's idea."

"He's worthless."

"No, he's the idea man," Phil said. "Our get-out-of-jail-free card. Barry will leave some samples here but he's not doing any flying for us if he sees we don't have a good game going on."

The crowd grew rowdier and Miguelito and Abner had to be broken up. The DJ put on some loud and metallic dub-reggae. Phil overheard Blitz by the DJ table doing a terrible island accent. Nobody laughed except his entourage: Sensation, Omar, and Hassle. "He doesn't understand how much that gets on my nerves," Phil said.

Reynolds' wife floated by, a light-eyed blonde whose shell-shocked face manifested the ghosts of her previous husbands. She'd been passed around by other men here, even Phil. Now, it was Reynolds' turn at her.

"These guns are a one-time deal," Reynolds said, no longer smiling at his wife. He just…let her float on by. She stared at Barry's well-manicured, sandaled feet and was out of sight for most of the party. Barry sat back, relaxing on a lounger while people stood over him.

Reynolds said, "Guess we'll be trading girls and meth out of Central Florida for the rest of our careers if this doesn't work out."

"Girls and drugs are keeping this shit afloat," Phil said. "How long, who knows? We either upgrade or bust. Barry's an asshole. Ever heard of keeping your enemies close? He's doing that with us right now."

"He's our only source for prime shit. We got no beef with him. Why's he feel that way?"

Phil shrugged. "Because he's an ornery motherfucker. He likes to play with the popular kids and feels we're not there yet. He can do whatever he wants. But starting today, we clean house. We want legitimacy? We have to clean it from the ground up. Starting with Billy. I wanna be there when it happens." Phil watched Barry stand up from the lounge chair, wearing shorts and an Acapulco shirt adorned with palms and hibiscus flowers. Loud and sweaty, throwing out one punchline after another.

"…Now she's sitting in a pile of shit," Barry said. "He asks, 'Why'd you do that?' and she goes, 'I'm too old to come, so I had to do *something*.'"

That set off a seismic rumble of laughter. Even Phil and Reynolds roared. They walked off and rounded the fence perimeter.

"Who are those two faggots over there?" Reynolds asked.

"Friends of Billy. Sub-sub," Phil said.

Strung out and wrung out, the duo approached them as if invited.

Reynolds brushed his hair back with one hand. "Ass-clowns. One of them showed me a picture of a man sucking his own cock."

"He was sucking his own cock?"

"I saw it with my own eyes."

"Goddamn. You didn't look away?" Phil asked.

"It doesn't make me a fag if I didn't." Reynolds crossed his arms. "How could I not look? This guy was all convoluted, slurping up his own tube."

"Who the fuck carries around something like that?" Phil smelled them on their approach. Pasty flesh and blotchy skin. Tracks up their arms. Smelled like they'd been living out of a van in the same socks and underwear for months. Looked like it too. Black, cum-stained clothes and ratty sneakers. Grungy hair. "Who invited you?" Phil asked, fanning his nose.

"We know about Billy's next party," Gay J, the taller of the two, said. The one with the runny nose.

Phil's eyes shifted between them. "I was just gonna ask. You want pills?"

"Blitz said we could hang," Gay J said.

"We're among friends," said Max.

"Friends?" Reynolds kidded. "You're not my friend, fag."

"Of course we're friends," Max said. "I shared that photo with you, man. Some guy gave me that in Texas when we were driving through."

They laughed, for once not at Barry's punchline. The bald and furry one had gone inside to face-ride some rails. Or perhaps to fuck Reynolds's wife in the upstairs bathroom.

Reynolds patted Max's shoulder while holding his nose. "Why don't we go party with you and Billy?"

"Depends whatchoo got for us," Max said.

"Hey, man." Gay J snorted. "If Blitz can be our steady plug, we'll tell you anything."

"That's what I like to hear," Reynolds said. "Without dedication, you ain't shit around here."

"But I really need a fix," Gay J said. "Like right now."

"You'll get it," Phil said.

"We been on the road, man," Gay J said. There was scruff growing over the acne he scratched.

"Oh yeah?" Reynolds snorted.

"Yeah." Max smiled, his eyes glossed with desperate glee. "We play in a band."

"What kind of music?"

"Well," Gay J said, "it's like really loud rock with screaming. We stare at our sneakers a lot."

Reynolds leaned between them. "Come around tomorrow and we'll hang out with Billy, okay?" He dropped some pills into their dirty hands and shooed them off.

When there was nothing more left to say, the dirty duo moved near the grill.

"That smoke ought to keep them from smelling so gamey," Phil said to Reynolds. "It'll cure them."

"Is that what that smell was?" Reynolds held his nose. "Goddamn."

Things got more sinister when the sun set. The party moved indoors. Louder, hazier. Strobing disco lights, everybody dancing. Phil had two stripper poles installed in the living room and the girls went to work. Barry took off all clothes except his white socks and danced with the girls. People fucked openly on couches.

"When you taking me to Mexico?" Phil asked Barry, off the dance floor.

"That depends, man," said Barry. "My schedule's gonna keep me flying all over the place over the next few weeks."

"Goddamn," Phil said. "That's why we need this partnership, man."

"I'm flying across the border, crop-dusting cocaine as I go. Let the natives know what a friendly guy I am."

"Sounds like we could use that here."

"Naw, man. This city hasn't earned that privilege."

"Yet," said Phil.

Barry grimaced. "Well, I'm not sure. We'll play it by ear, as they say."

They laughed and carried on. Later that night and into morning, Reynolds drove his drunk wife home along with Phil, Abner, and Miguelito. His car was as big as a boat and just as accommodating. Reynolds carried her in and left her on the sofa. He was back in the car, sober but smoking a joint. Driving through the humid night to drop the rest of them off.

# CH. NINE

She was in parties. She was in parties. She *was* parties.

Jubilee's first night out of the clinic. Inconceivably high, running around Nikki's house naked, rubbing paint all over each other to give them an excuse to jump into the pool, making complete fools of themselves. Mari was in on it too. She'd later recount that this stupefied period of her life was peak euphoria. Dressing up with whatever was around, setting up situations and skits, and mocking others who weren't in on it. Mari kissed her for the first time that night. Jubilee brought a dump truck of unnecessary drama and little else. No weed, no pills. Not even a purse. Fights broke out and they ran out on bar tabs. None of the mockery or pointing fingers mattered because Mari and Jubilee had found each other. Mari almost believed she was in love. Silly girls giggling was sometimes love.

Nikki wore a red wedding gown tonight. Mari could see it a block away, even in the dark. Shiny, tacky, hilarious. From the far end of the strip, The Garage blared sounds of the '80s: Devo, Bananarama, The Police, Flock of Seagulls.

"Bitch, you didn't wear the dress we bought!" Nikki said. 19-years-old, a voluptuous horror of ghoulish aesthetic: black makeup around her eyes and dusty dreadlocks knotted with neon thread. She worked the door, trading cash for tickets and the occasional fistful of pills. "You look like Tank Girl in those shorts and boots, Mari. I thought you would have at least worn your tux..."

"I don't have a tux," Mari said, slowly approaching, nervously holding herself. Outside The Garage, kids between the ages of 14 and 20 hopped about, talking, dancing, smoking, laughing. Mari felt old around them.

"You're late." Nikki's voice boomed as loud as her bright white face, boobs bouncing with their own agenda, overflowing from the top of her gown.

Standing beside her, Mari was thin and masculine. "This music sucks," Mari said.

"You don't dance anyway," Nikki sassed.

"I hate Tommy Tutone."

Nikki gasped and squeezed her arm. "But that's the music of our childhood!"

"I don't know what you remember from your childhood but, for me, it wasn't this shit."

"Mari." Nikki put an arm around her as they went inside. "Why do you always overanalyze shit? Calm the fuck down."

"You're the spaz, bitch. How many did you take?"

"None of your fucking business. You're always so moody and judgmental. And you're late as fuck. They ate all the sandwiches."

"Where's Jubilee?"

"Haven't seen her. Haven't even heard from her." Nikki looked up and winked at a guy wearing a gorilla mask.

"You think she might make it to her own birthday party," Mari said.

"What a bitch, huh?"

Mari shook her head, surveying the happening.

"You two are like sisters," Nikki said. "Scissor sisters."

"I'm leaving."

"Wait. You planned this whole thing. She'll be bummed out if you go."

"Nikki, she's not even here! Jesus!"

"Is she mad at you?"

"For what?" Mari stared at her.

"She's mad at you for something. Says you nag her like her mom."

"She barely knew her mom so she's full of shit," Mari said. "And if she actually listened to what I said, she wouldn't be broke and homeless. Again. God, what a stupid bitch."

Nikki gave her a more serious look. "Honey, that's mean."

"Well, it's how I feel. She doesn't even realize the reason for all her failings is because she won't fucking listen to me."

"Are you going to tell her that when you see her? Probably not."

"I can tell she's pissed when she doesn't call me."

They entered the gala and Nikki dragged Mari around the dance floor. Kids danced beneath a disco ball to "Something There to Remind Me." The sidelines crowded with freaks and geeks drinking spiked punch while chit-chatting. There was a pillow fight in one corner. Younger girls still in high school. Fake IDs and fake ambitions. Small girls grooved like roly-poly trolls. Fizzed-out raspberry hair on one, short two-toned blonde on another. Tiny backpacks, sucking on lollipops and pacifiers.

"I'm going to Austin like next month," the raspberry one said.

Mari caught part of the conversation, moving along the outer dance floor.

"You don't have money," Two-Toned Blonde said.

"I been cutting hair."

"Yeah, but you're not certified. Plus, you fucked up the back of my head."

"That's 'cause your head's misshapen."

"It's not. And you fucked up that tattoo on my foot."

"That was a practice one. Hire a professional next time. I'm going to cosmo school when I get to Austin."

"Makeup?"

"Not just that. Hair. Coloring."

"Ooh, learn nails so you can do mine."

"How am I supposed to do yours when I'm in Austin?"

"You won't go."

"Why not?"

"Because that's what you always say. And here you are, time and again."

"God, is there food here?"

"I think somebody's been licking the BBQ chips. They're soggy."

"Gross. Hey, Duckface Debbie is here. Keep your shit close. She's a fucking klepto that stole from the church plate when I was little."

"Jubilee too..."

"She just got out of rehab. I didn't bring a gift or nothing..."

"I heard she found Jesus..."

Nikki broke away from Mari, searching faces. Blending in, dancing. She drank sports drinks spiked with grain alcohol and Oxy. Hillbilly heroin, the kids called it.

Laughing and joking in the corner with Billy Zombie was Jubilee. Long and scrawny, boyish like Edie Sedgwick, only ethnic. Billy Zombie was a trust-fund kid emaciated by vice. Blackened teeth, limp arms but always a grin. Always talking like he was halfway through a punchline and couldn't stop giggling. Dull eyes half-closed.

But even as a somnambulant freak, he was aware of his surroundings and all the leeches slurping at him. He spotted Mari coming towards them and pointed her out to Jubilee. She handed her cigarette to him and threw herself at Mari, arms open. She strangled more than embraced, junkie arms squeezing the life out of Mari. They investigated each other's faces. Jubilee's eyes were vacant.

Mari whispered in her ear, "Glad you made it to your own birthday party."

"What?!" Jubilee cackled.

Mari's approach was at first intimate. Jubilee could easily crush it and throw it all away.

"Thank you, thank you! Honey, this is a great party!"

"How'd you get here?" Mari held her around the waist. They looked conjoined, but one looked sicker than the other.

Jubilee flipped her thumb at Billy Zombie, who was grinning in the corner. She shrugged.

"You're still fucking around with him," Mari said and let her go.

"Fucking him?"

"Don't get so loud. I didn't say *fucking him*."

Jubilee laughed. "He can't even get it up. He just gives me stuff."

"One day, he'll exhaust it all. Or the soul-suckers that surround him will take it all from him," Mari said. "Who are you going to go to next? You know you'll wind up coming right back to me. I'm always your safety net."

"So, stop being so nice to me. And I won't come back."

"What? Fuck you. I'm the only one looking out for you."

"What did I tell you about reminding me?" Jubilee said. She reached out for her. "Like I owe you something? You're not the only one looking out for me."

"Drug freaks don't count," Mari said. She wanted to be in her arms again. "If you want to talk, let's go talk over there...away from this fucking creep. You wanna go back to the clinic? You want me to get a power of attorney?"

"No," Jubilee said. "And you'd never. That's such a trashy thing to say. How could you think that?"

They crossed the dancefloor to the other side of the hangar-like Garage. Some kids had crashed on beanbags, draped all over each other, drooling. In the dark, Mari grabbed her and smothered her lips. It didn't matter that Jubilee's mouth smelled like burnt sugar. Jubilee wrapped one leg around Mari's skinny ones and ground into her. Mari kissed her neck, caressing the back of her head. Jubilee's hair was now earlobe-length, dirty, and unruly with a white skunk-streak running down the middle. They danced around, holding each other tight around the waist.

"I haven't felt anything like this in a while." Jubilee pulled away but held Mari's hands.

Mari pulled her back. "Brought you back to life?" Mari asked. "When was the last time you took a hit?"

The shared sensation had nothing to do with narcotics. Mari knew it, but Jubilee could not put it into words: the electric current running between them, blue and static. The feeling of being alive without the frisson of drugs. The nervous fluttering in their stomachs, the gleam in their eyes.

"I'm already fucking pissed," Mari said. "You were close to six months clean, baby. Six fucking months that you've flushed away. I told you I didn't want you hanging out with him."

"Billy?" Jubilee said. "He's fucking harmless. You only know him from that one time. That's why you hate him."

"What about those people around him?" Mari said. They were face to face. Mari stroked her cheek and brow with the back of her hand.

"He's a rich kid. Sometimes it's just a bunch of jocks that want to buy pills. But they're all his friends."

"Goddamn it, Jubilee... I miss you."

"I know." Her face was a mask of culpability. "I'm sorry. I miss you, too."

"It's your fucking birthday and I thought you weren't going to show up."

"I've been here a while. Nikki probably didn't see me, that's all. And you're the one that got here late. So maybe you don't know what the hell you're talking about."

"What happened to you showing up for dinner?" asked Mari. "I cooked for you."

"I don't eat. I forgot. I'm sorry."

"You know how sick I am about this?"

"I'm so sorry. Please tell me you love me."

Mari backed away and looked suspiciously at her. Jubilee would never mock her like this. "Convince me that I should."

"*Hmm*, Billy is throwing me an after-party at his pad."

"At his parents' house?"

"Oh, no. It's at his place. And his place is the shit. It's one of those new condos near the bay. He's got the floor to himself. How about that for good times?" Jubilee teasingly ran a finger from Mari's neck to her chin. "Come with me? Might help to keep me out of trouble if you do."

"You're fucking right, I'm going. And then you're coming home with me."

"Okay," Jubilee said. "But, we can prolly crash there tonight. Glad we can do this together."

Mari convinced herself to go with it, no matter how blind it made her. This would be the last time. She'd grown tired of her junkie girlfriend.

# CH. TEN

A most profound sleep. Near-death.

Mari woke with a deep sigh. He'd startled her, punching the door open when he returned to the room. Her heart was in her throat. Rising off the pillow, her hair was in good shape, considering. She hadn't felt more awake than that moment.

"Lucky it was me and not Blitz or his homies," Phil said. He was a silhouette and she could not recall his face but could feel his smirk. "I bet your butthole is sore."

Mari closed her shirt with one hand, grabbed the gun he'd forgotten on the night table, turned her face, closed her eyes, and shot him.

Sometime in the night, he'd crawled over her, smelling of faded cologne, mud, and something so unpleasant that she knew only as male pheromone. He'd gotten into it like he was doing her a favor, asking if she was enjoying it, placing a gun to her head. When he'd finished, he'd left the room for a nightcap, returning this morning.

After the blast, she opened her eyes, jumped out of bed, and gathered her clothes, which had been scattered all over the small room. She dressed and walked over him. He had a big hole in his face where his eye and part of his forehead had been. Part of his ear was gone too. Skin and hair flapped over in the gathered blood.

There would be a car waiting downstairs. Reynolds or any of those creeps waiting at the wheel. She exited through the pool deck onto an alley, having no sense of where she was or what day it was. Still in Carbon, by the smell. Small city but sprawled. Populated centrally by blacks and Hispanics but controlled by descendants of the Confederacy. That was everything she needed to know about Carbon.

Memories came with the sparkle and throb of a migraine. She'd been taken out of Billy Zombie's loft and thrown into the trunk of a car. Later that day, she explained it to Kika over coffee.

The streets near the landfill looked like post-apocalyptic Tijuana. The morning fog mingled with the smoke of smoldering garbage fires. A sad-eyed dog limped past her like he was hurrying out of town.

Mari pulled Jubilee's phone out of her pocket and hoped. Willed it to ring. To hear anything. She'd tucked the gun into the back of her waistband, having never held or carried a weapon before. It felt cold and heavy near her ass crack, sending a chill up her spine to her stiffening neck.

With the sun behind her, she walked, arms folded over her chest. The phone in her back pocket suddenly vibrated. Her relief was audible to the woman who called.

# CH. ELEVEN

Kika sat in the last booth in the back, wearing a black dress, sunglasses. She smelled of fresh soap.

"I didn't expect a Chinese girl," she said. In the shadow of the booth, she looked older, sinister. Witchy. Darker than the picture Jubilee had shown Mari.

"I'm not Chinese," Mari said. "I'm a mutt. My dad was Vietnamese, and my mom was Mexican, from Texas."

"*¿Hablas español?*" Kika asked.

"I have to, around here."

"Bet you get asked that a lot."

Mari nodded. "Can I sit?"

Kika waved her hand over the table.

The more Mari searched her face, the more Kika shrunk into the shadow.

"Jubilee never mentioned you," Kika said.

"She told me she had a sister she didn't talk to very often."

"Hardly at all, actually."

"Oh. You used to live here, then. Both of you grew up here, right? Then you…left. I didn't expect you'd come looking for her."

"I came to take her away."

Mari marinated those words. She touched the soft skin of her own face, monitoring the empty diner. "I wanted to take her away and I couldn't," Mari said. "It's been days since I last saw her. She infuriates me with the shit she does. Now I wish for… I just want her back. Fuck. Some really bad shit happened."

The cook came out of the kitchen to serve them coffee. At the rate Kika was drinking it, he decided to leave the decanter at the table. Kika ordered something hardy and heavy for them to eat.

"Where does she usually go?" Kika asked. "Where's the rat hole in a rat-hole town?"

"They took her," said Mari. "She could be anywhere." She muted her sob with the back of her hand. She felt too tired to cry. "This isn't even a real town. It's more of an annex that Woodbine abandoned. It's White Oak's toilet now. No mayor. And if there was a city hall, it'd be occupied with drug dealers, pimps, and hookers."

"They don't put landfills on maps," said Kika.

"Will you help me look for her? We're pretty much broken up now, I guess. But I need to make sure she's okay before I get the fuck out of town."

"This ship sank a long time ago."

"I know. I tried to help. I stayed too long. Where do you plan on taking her?"

Kika surveyed the parking lot through the glass pane. "Where I should have taken her a long time ago but couldn't. I bailed on her when they took me away. I abandoned her."

"Her life's just spiraled uncontrollably, in and out of chaos," Mari said. "You were her only protection, the only family until I met her. She said you were in prison…"

"That's what they say," Kika said. "But it wasn't prison. It was confinement away from here. From her. From myself."

"I did everything I could." Mari pinched her lips, shaking her head. "But she is who she is. Whatever I do is never enough to keep her safe."

The cook brought their hot plates out and Mari forked eggs, potatoes, sausage, and bacon into her mouth while Kika watched, occasionally picking from her own plate and drinking coffee.

# CH. TWELVE

The birthday party raged on that night with them loitering in a fast-food parking lot, ending with a French fry and milkshake fight. After splattering each other and the cars around them, they piled into a tiny Ford Escort and sped off, giggling on a cloud of laughing gas. After an hour of cruising and mindlessly circling, they wound up at a miniature golf course. Mari downed half a bottle of whiskey in one gulp while inside the car. Someone vomited out the window then swigged from the same bottle.

Mari laughed so hard, she threw up as she climbed out of the car.

"This is breaking and entering," she said.

"It ain't if you got the keys." Billy Zombie led them through the fence gate and around the miniature course. Some of them had already jumped the fence, dancing across the field. Nikki looked aflame, tangoing in that crazy wedding dress. Garden gnomes and plastic pirates saluted them on the concrete walk. Strange ceramic statues grinned behind plastic trees.

"Jubilee," Billy said. "Tell your girl to chill."

"What?" Mari was abuzz. "Who, me?"

Jubilee turned to Mari and said, "Relax. His parents own the place."

Just then, the sprinklers turned on. Everybody stripped down to their dingy underwear except Mari, who stood with her arms crossed, pacing back and forth under the sprinkler rain. They scrubbed the milkshake residue off each other and sprinted across the course. Then they went crawling through a maze of buccaneers, then a tunnel of skeleton sailors, and finally a group of plaster clowns. Some guy in a gorilla mask swung from a rope, dangling off the mast of a pirate ship built into to a plaster waterfall. They fell over laughing, then tumbled over to the ball cage. After grabbing handfuls of golf balls, they threw a hailstorm over the acreage in a spontaneous throwing contest. When they heard a window shatter in the distance, they ran back to the clubhouse and dried off. They raided the snack machine, leaving wrappers, crumbs, and half-eaten candy bars on the carpet. When they eventually left, Billy forgot to turn off the sprinklers and houselights. Eventually, the neighbors called the cops but, by then, they were all at Billy Zombie's loft on the fourth floor overlooking Carcass Bay, the strip, and the landfill.

Jubilee turned 23 the day she met Blitz Davis. Mari could no longer keep up with her that night. Could no longer keep her safe.

People came and went out of the giant loft. Sections of the commodious apartment were separated by temporary walls, each a different color like Prince Prospero's abbey. One room glowed volcanic red from multiple lava lamps. There was an all-black room and an all-white room with blood-paint handprints on the walls and ceiling. S&M chains draped the walls of a blue room and a sex swing dangled from the rafters.

"No one really uses it," someone whispered to Mari when she inspected it.

Techno beats looped ad nauseam from overhead speakers. Strobes pulsated. Skinny, naked girls frugged under twinkling, mirrored balls. A covey of giggling miscreants sat in front of a widescreen TV, watching *Man Bites Dog*, but they were distracted. Too lazy to read subtitles. Mari went into a smoky room where Jubilee spun around a pole, wearing a plastic, green cowboy hat. She'd replaced her sweaty tank top with a fringed leather vest. By the time Mari circled around to her, Jubilee had vanished. There were small clusters of people in all the rooms. Strangers.

People she met suddenly vanished minutes later. New ones appeared from nowhere as if they'd entered through some other-dimensional portal. The closets were all stuffed and overcrowded with spinning, grinning sexcapades.

The Doritos had all gone soggy in their giant bowl. The dip was warm and had most likely been there for days. Warm soda, cheap beer. The loft had a sinister pulse all its own. The walls breathed but Mari felt suffocated. The room spun. The ceiling stretched into a flexible bouncy house dome. The floor dropped 100 feet beneath her. By some misguided direction, she entered the kitchen and rummaged through the fridge. She found empty Chinese takeaway containers and a carton of sour milk. In the freezer, there was Everclear. She drank a shot and then another. There was some sort of purple juice in a tumbler. She mixed the two. It was like drinking fuel and chasing it with mouthwash.

When she woke up an hour later, she was sitting in front of the kitchen sink with her knees at her chest. Music still blaring. Strobes opened a portal where they'd all lost their minds. She crawled around the loft on her knees until she found a mattress in one of the sectioned rooms. She needed to put her head down. Get some sort of rest between dimensions. Her head was full of sounds and voices in her sleep.

"You're jealous, aren't you?"

"Why?"

"Because, since The Garage, everyone's been flirting with me."

Daylight arrived, seemed like weeks later. Mari woke up in a corner of the room, all by herself. Or was it the day after that? Hipster ephemera cluttered the room: postcards of The Rolling Stones, Jane's Addiction, and New Order; compact discs, cassette tapes, a broken guitar, and magazines stacked on top of stereos and turntables. Water pipes had tipped over and stained the carpet with black resin juice. Early morning murmur had woken her. She drooled all over the sheet and the arm she'd used as a pillow. Noticing its sour smell, she sat up. Her tongue was swollen, she tasted blood. Her anus felt sore. Her breasts and nipples hurt. She repositioned herself, but it was apparent there had been an intrusion. She had on underwear and a tank top and nothing else, neither of which belonged to her. Her shaky hands reached down and explored. She brought up her fingers and smelled them. There was no blood from either orifice, but she definitely needed to wash.

Too scared to get up.

*Whump whump whump.* The ceiling fan twirled.

The surroundings slowly came into focus one section at a time. She pressed back her urge to call out to anyone who might've been hanging around. She moved to the edge of the partition.

There were voices in the hallway.

# CH. THIRTEEN

"I was volunteering at the rehab when I met her," Mari told Kika. "Everyone in this town has a habit and addiction."

"I can tell you're not from around here," said Kika. "You actually care. My sister has a way of leeching onto good people when she's desperate."

"She said you'd say that."

"All I wanted was to escape Carbon, no matter how. I imagine Jubi was brought to your clinic against her will."

"Our friend Nikki drove her there. Kicking and screaming."

"And you eventually convinced her that she was okay under the condition that you'd look after her."

"Yeah. I guess I convinced her. I did a shitty job protecting her… Hey, I need a smoke."

"No, not yet. We're not finished."

# H.

# DIA DE PUERCOS

# CH. ONE

"Yo, bro, we go way back. There's no need for hostility."

"This place looks like the set of a porno. Smells like it."

Voices, right in the next room. Mari had pressed close to the partition wall, heard all of it like they'd been in the room with her.

"Billy, Billy, Billy." A robust but calm voice, chuckling. The sound of pounded flesh was sickening. She covered her ears. "Shame on us because we really had some high expectations of you. Billy, this is really our fault, so I want you to forgive us."

Billy screamed, "I forgive you, man! I forgive you! Stop punching me!"

Mari pressed as close to the partition as she could. There was a full-length mirror nailed to the opposite wall and, when she positioned her head just right, the angle afforded their reflection. They'd easily see her, so she moved over as far as she could, steadying her breathing, keeping very still. She made out two men standing over Billy, one of them holding him around the neck with his large hand. Billy's bruised face was soaked with tears, dirty hands shaking at them, pleading.

The beefy guy holding him slapped the back of his head repeatedly. He said, "So, let me understand this: You don't have the blow, but you don't have the money either. Billy, this is going to sound stupid, but do you remember who we are? We gave that to you in good faith because you've been so good to us. I mean, you're our number one customer. Now I realize: You crashed on your own stash. You forgot, you're not supposed to smash on your stash, man. You should have just taken the money and run. Or leave part of the stash, or step on it a few more times and pay it back."

"I did step on it," Billy said. "B-But we used it all up."

"You dumb son of a bitch," the guy said. "You don't wait around for us to show up. That's just fucking lazy, man. And you wanna stay in business with us?"

"Yeah, I do. You guys have a good thing going, ya know?" Billy's tears washed lines through the grime and grit of his face.

"Of course, we do." Another guy spoke. "Billy. You didn't even invite us to your party!"

"S-Sorry."

"But Billy, you kind of screwed us," the first guy said.

Billy shouted, "S-Sometimes I think you fuckers want us to run off with your shit just so you can come after us!"

"Shut up!" the first guy said.

"Take it easy," someone else whispered. He had boss status, wearing a blue suit with the sleeves pulled up to the elbow.

She'd seen him. His face. Eventually, she saw all their faces.

"Billy, what's this 'us' you keep referring to?" The first guy again. "You mean the low guys? There's no 'us' because no one is ever stupid enough to pull off what you did. And what the fuck do you have to show for it? A big, shitty party with a bunch of bugged-out girls? A bunch of queers having a nap after an all-nighter? Huh? You trying to impress a bunch of junkies, you stupid piece of shit? You're just a trust-fund kid. Don't ever forget that."

"So, you did it for street-cred, was that it?" the boss said. "You wouldn't make it one week out there with us, Billy."

"Of course, we have to come down hard on you." The first guy again. He, of lectures and unnecessary roughness. "The standard operation goes as such: I'm going to ask you some questions. Very basic questions. You won't need to know anything about science or physics. These are more common-sense questions. First one is… Since you don't have our stash—and a small stash, it was—where's the money? If the money is here, then your problems are reduced. If there is no stash and no cash, which is what we're praying isn't the case, then Billy, we will have to take a trip."

"Aw, no. Not a trip! Please, no."

Blitz Davis stepped into the reflection. Another henchman dragged someone from the other side of the hallway. Jubilee. They threw her on the sofa next to Billy Zombie.

"Look what I found," a woman said. A brusque, broad woman, sporting a similar suit as the boss, with short, cartoonish yellow hair. "She's sweet. A little dirty but sweet." She had a Carolina accent. "I want to take her with me and pet her all day long."

"Ew, cut that shit out," Blitz told her. "Keep that shit out of my sight!"

"Hey, fuck you! What'd I say about talking to me like that?"

Blitz turned to the boss. "Phil, you're going to let her talk to me like that?"

"Shut the fuck up!" the woman responded and there was some shuffling around the carpet.

Billy cried into his lap. Mari couldn't see Jubilee too well but heard her trying to calm things in her casually stoned demeanor.

"Listen, both of you, cool your shit," Phil said. "We're here about this zombie freak, nobody else. Billy, it's up to you, man. You decide, right here, right now."

"I decide not to die," Billy screamed, snot streaming over his pencil-thin mustache.

"Hey, you guys, cool it," Jubilee said in a tone Mari would have used on her. "Let's discuss this calmly over some coffee. Smoke a joint, relax. It's too early for this shit. Nobody has to get hurt."

"You keep quiet," the woman in the suit shouted in her face.

"Just chill," Jubilee said. "I'll make some coffee and then—"

The woman shut her down with a backhand.

"Well, Billy," the first guy said. "It's the package or the cash. It doesn't work if you ain't got the do-re-mi."

Billy's face melted like a televangelist's wife. "I don't have any of it... How could you be so stupid as to give a junkie that much coke...and expect to get a profit back on it? It's your fucking fault."

"We wanted to clean you up," Phil said. "I did this as an act of trust and look how it turned out. Billy, it means we can't trust you anymore. Nothing personal. It was a test. Failure is painful, Billy. Look, I'm sick of this shit. Take them out of here."

There was a struggle and Billy shrieked like a wounded puppy until they taped up his mouth.

"What about the girl?" the woman asked.

Now they'd all pulled away from the reflection to the center of the other room.

"What do you want to do with her?" Blitz asked.

"I don't want to go!" This was the first time Mari had ever heard panic in Jubilee's voice. "Please!"

Mari bit her lip, covering her mouth to keep from crying.

"C'mon, honey, you ride with me," the woman said and lifted her in a fireman's hold.

Jubilee struggled but was too frail.

Phil and the other tough worked Billy over until they were satisfied and then hauled him off. They vacated quickly, leaving the front door of the apartment open. Mari heard the tide in the distance. It was overcast, the sky was white and yellow like soured milk. She waited and waited, slumped on the floor, biting her thumbnail.

She'd dozed off before a rude awakening: a hand over her mouth, she was quickly scooped off the floor. A firm grip on her thigh and another on her buttock as Reynolds lifted her over his shoulder and carried her outside. The salty air was chill, and she couldn't help but urinate down his shoulder when she was brought down to the car.

All she could see were dirty loafers. Their owners laughed at Reynolds and he cursed and pinched her.

"Throw her in Embra's trunk," Phil told him. She could smell his cologne but couldn't see his face.

"But I want her," Reynolds said.

"Dude, you're married," Phil said. "Throw her in there. Geez, I guess we're running out of room."

"In that case, you dispatch her."

"You don't know what I'm doing so put her in and shut the fuck up. Embra, follow me."

More laughs except Reynolds. Grumbling, he tossed her in a small, white sports car. Her head hit the edge of the trunk and it got dark. She felt her arms go limp as she fell into darkness, deep into a black crevice of unconsciousness and probable death. She awoke when Phil busted into the hotel room because he'd forgotten his gun on the nightstand after he'd dressed.

# CH. TWO

"I live, always expecting the worst. The rest isn't so bad," Kika said when Mari had told her what happened after the party. "Prepare for the worst and what comes next isn't so bad."

Mari could see more than half her face now. She looked exactly like Jubilee but older, with longer, shinier hair. Slim but muscular. Large hands. Her arms bruised and scratched, wrists deeply cut. Tattoos covering up a skinscape of scars.

Their eyes locked for that moment. Mari looked up from her arms. Kika stared deeply into her. Mari rolled her eyes when she could no longer hold her gaze.

"You keep looking around," Kika said. "Stop acting so paranoid. I'm not going to hurt you."

"Fuck. Guess I'm scared shitless," Mari said. "I pissed them off. I did some damage along the way. I don't think I can be out in the open too long. I shot a man."

"Did you kill him?"

"I guess I did. I wasn't aiming to. I just shot. I didn't stick around for the autopsy."

"Killing gets easier with practice."

# CH. THREE

That same morning, Detective Funzo was going to keep driving until he fell off the flat earth surface, but now saw two shapes walking ahead in the early morning smog and slowed down. The path was a toxic, two-lane drive carved out near the Carbon exit off 380. The sun struggled through the clouds, giving the landscape a pinkish, rusty tinge. Breathing around here gave him a sore throat.

Cleaning fluid spat across the dusty windshield, followed by the drone of wipers. He parked the car and watched the two shapes approach. Eventually, they became recognizable forms. He rubbed his eyes, squinting. Hadn't slept in 30 hours. He pulled his service revolver out of the holster in his coat and stuck it in his side pocket. He zipped up his pants, wiping his hand on the side of the gray trench coat. Rolled up the windows and stepped out of the car.

"Look at this dream team." Funzo approached them, black Oxford shoes grinding gravel. "You two crawling out of town? One can only hope."

Blitz Davis stopped and sat on the curb, holding the last drops of whiskey in a bottle. Yumi, the Thai hooker with the blue wig, stood over him, stockings torn, knees bleeding. She looked at Funzo, twisting bubblegum out of her mouth.

"Fuck you." Blitz balanced his middle finger up at him.

"It's been a real fucked up morning, asshole," Funzo said.

"I can tell," Blitz said. "You smell like her." He gestured toward his companion.

She kicked gravel at him and paced across the street, then back. Humming to herself.

"You know where Philip is?" Funzo asked.

"How the fuck should I know," Blitz said. He looked up with one eye closed. "Call his office."

"When was the last time you saw him?"

"Shit, probably the last time you saw him."

"Yeah? Well, then I'm the first to tell you that he was just rolled out of a hotel off the strip this morning. Shot in the face. Doesn't look like he's going to come out of this one with a smile."

Blitz's face twisted. He closed his eyes, ran a hand through his stylish hair. "I'm really fucked up right now." He coughed and his face crinkled into a crying fit. Lasted all of two minutes. He wiped his eyes, stuck a cigarette in his mouth, took a long drag. "I'm trying to make sense out of what you just said. What the fuck happened?"

"I'll tell you what else fucking happened," Funzo said. "Your crew. All dead. Slashed and beaten…" He looked at Yumi. "Sweetheart, when was the last time you saw those motherfuckers?"

Yumi stopped in the middle of the road, made a confused clown face, and shook her head.

Funzo waved a hooked finger back at his car. "Let's the three of us get in and go for a drive. Now."

The champagne-colored, unmarked Buick faded into the morning dust, heading back to the main strip. "Downtown:" four stumpy business buildings, a short line of bars, churches, casinos, and strip clubs. Shuttered businesses awaiting contracts that would never get signed.

Slowly driving past the smoldering storefront, Funzo waved at the fireman who was rolling up the last hose.

"What the fuck happened to the club?" Blitz asked from the passenger side, rubbing his burning eyes.

"Don't have details," said Funzo. "Supposedly happened around the same time as the attack on your boys."

Blitz licked the scruffy corner of his lip.

Funzo held the wheel with one hand and suddenly punched Blitz in the face with the other. Yumi laughed.

"Motherfucker," Blitz yelled, pressing his cheek.

"Are you awake yet?" Funzo's lips curled over his yellow teeth. "'Cause I'll stick my fist up your fucking ass next. That'll wake you up!"

Blitz growled, clenching his fists. "God! Okay! What the fuck is wrong with you?"

"What?" Funzo said. "What? You're gonna hit a cop? Fuck off, asshole. All the bullshit I have to deal with to cover up this fucking mess and you're out fucking around like it's New Year's Eve. I always thought that if the whole shithouse went up, you'd be the first to go. They got to Philip first. And then your boys."

"Not Jamaicans though." Blitz stroked his scruff. "Jamaicans? Why is it always Jamaicans?"

"I never said that," said Funzo. "But they're on the top of the list because of this business you got pending with them. Even Mexicans won't come into Carbon because it smells like shit. This town has nothing. The Jamaicans see that, and they want to move in. Clean it up and claim it. Right here under our noses."

Blitz rubbed his neck. "All three of my boys? Sensation and Hassle? Turtlehead Omar? I bought them drinks at the club last night. We did lots of shots. I didn't ride with them, though. I don't think so, anyway."

"You didn't, I swear," said Yumi.

"Yeah, what she said," Blitz said.

Funzo looked at him. "Why didn't you drive?"

"Had to meet up with Phil. I was too fucked up afterwards."

"Never stopped you before. Did you see anyone new come into town? Any strangers you didn't recognize? Anybody in the club that wasn't some frat boy? Any niggers?"

"Man, you know how it is," Blitz said. "People in and out of Carbon. There's two things people come here for. If it wasn't for drug and pussy tourism, we wouldn't be here. How am I supposed to know every stranger that comes through?"

"Not that you'd remember anyway, you fucking lush."

"Hey, come on, man. It was the usual nightly crowd, most from out of town. I don't know any of them. And niggers don't do shit like this."

"Did you see any Jamaicans, stupid?"

"Nah, man," Blitz said. "Why does it have to be them? I think I would know if I saw them. Ain't you the detective? I don't know nothing."

Funzo slowly drove past the building. "Who've you been fucking around with? Who?"

"Fucking around with?" repeated Blitz. "Um, everybody? I go through about thirty chickenheads a week."

"Did you hold back on a delivery? Hold off on payment? What's happening? Did Philip talk to you about what he was doing?"

"Yeah. No. Sure. He has a bunch of things planned, so I don't know what you mean."

"The gun trade," said Funzo.

"We're waiting for the buyers to come in with the cash. We got all the shit they asked for, they just have to come pick it up."

"You know these people? You really, really know them?"

"Seth and Phil said they came with legit references," Blitz said. "I don't deal with that shit. They cut that deal."

"So, nobody suspicious or scheming? Huh? Seen anybody who doesn't belong?"

"Dude, Carbon is filled with nothing but scheming, shysty motherfuckers. Everybody knows this is Sodom and Gomorrah in the south. Only reason to come here is to roll, fuck in the street, or get murdered. You want to find whoever did this, keep doing what you're doing. This is why we pay you. You're the detective. Stop asking me all this stupid shit! You figure it out!"

"And I'm due for a raise," Funzo said. "Sure, I work the investigations and fill out false reports. You wanna know something? I got a big broom that sweeps all your shit under the carpet. This is a territorial pissing, is what it is. And now your guard is down, and you're going to have all sorts of creeps coming in, sniffing around, seeing what they can take. And you motherfuckers aren't even ready! You don't have the manpower."

"We're talking it all out, man," Blitz said. "We do it all the time. Reynolds has it under control. Seth and Phil planned it all out."

"Yeah, they'll talk it out by burning the rest of this fucking town while you're out partying. I'll be the first one to pull out of this shithole when it gets taken over by a bunch of island niggers."

Blitz looked at him. He rubbed his face. "All right. This is too much to take in right now. Gimme a fucking break."

"Wake up," Funzo said. "Phil's dead. Let that sink in, shit heel. And fuck you. I've milked everything I could from this shithole, thinking that just maybe I can take a little piece with me when I retire. Turns out I got nothing. If things keep going on this messy trajectory, guess what?"

"You're moving to your mother's place in Florida? You been promising that for years, Detective. Yeah, you pull out now and you'll regret it."

"Don't you fucking threaten me, shit heel. I'll pistol-whip you and leave you where I found you."

Blitz shook his head, raising both hands in defeat.

"Honey, relax." Yumi massaged Funzo from the backseat. She was squeaky and cute like a cartoon. "You're going to blow up your heart. Take it easy."

"Get off me," Funzo said. He made a U-turn and headed back the way he'd driven, waving at random cops and firemen.

# CH. FOUR

"What I'm telling you is…" Seth said, leaning into the glass four stories above Carcass Bay. His voice was thick but high. Slightly nasally. Like a movie trailer announcer. "If some shit starts up, I want to know I'm covered. Shit is going to get gritty real soon. But it'll be over quickly. It'll pass."

"I saw the fire, if that's what you mean," Reynolds' voice echoed from Seth's desk-phone speaker. What Seth couldn't tell was that Reynolds didn't want to hear it. Not from the lawyer. The guy was a limp-dick, ex-frat boy Phil had grown up with, who could barely make it as an attorney in Florida. "My first thought was that it was a kitchen fire. But the kitchen's been closed for months. Plus, it was obviously a cocktail thrown through the window. Could be a random thing. Philip let Blitz ruin the place. That fucking kid does nothing but create more work for me."

"For us," Seth corrected.

There it was. The condescension.

"Right," said Reynolds.

"This is just a safety precaution," Seth said. "Better to be preemptive. You know what that means, right?"

Reynolds cleared his throat. "I ain't stupid, in case you're asking."

"You got tools?"

"They're in a safe location."

"Not what's in the crates. For your crew, I mean."

"We got it covered. On my way to pick up some extra help."

"Don't take from the stash. The trade is happening real soon."

"I'm not an idiot," Reynolds said. "I'm not taking from the arsenal. We got stashes for situations like this. And nobody gets a piece until I say so."

"Well, they better know," Seth said. "Shit just got real. They killed three of them. Slit their main veins."

Reynolds cleared his throat. "Cut their cocks off, huh?"

"No. Cut behind their knees and their carotid. Bled to death but not before getting their faces slashed up. They were robbed too."

"So, you don't know about Philip?"

"Know what? What happened?"

"Shot in the face."

"Fuck." Seth choked up. "Fuck! When?"

"This morning. Motel off the highway."

"Jesus. The same group?"

"Maybe. Too early to know who," Reynolds said. "We cleaned it up. Funeral is next week, after we get this business settled. Maybe it was some crackhead off the strip. Couldn't be that cunt he was with. You're gonna have to make the meeting on your own."

"Right after the raid at Billy's," Seth droned.

Reynolds could hear the bullshit gears grinding to produce a list of random conclusions.

"I don't know," Seth said. "Seems precise. Planned. No crackhead can pull off something like that. Burned the club and killed Phil, all in the same night. Coincidence? Hmm... This is a signal that there's other shit about to happen."

"It's good to be ready, then," Reynolds said.

"Obviously. Check around. Could be Barry."

"Funzo's on it. And Barry's too high-end to want this shit. Trust me. It's not like him."

"Well, get it together, my man. Tell them it could be war coming. It's in your court now. Let me know."

*Click.*

Reynolds looked at his phone, where he was sitting in his car, and gave it the finger.

# CH. FIVE

There was but the steam of coffee between the two women.

"How long did you work at the clinic?" Kika inched out of the shadow.

"It was part of my internship," Mari said. "The last two years or so."

"This town has a university?"

"No. But it was the closest place I could find outside White Oak."

"You came to do community service out of the kindness of your heart. Saving the world, one sister at a time? Cleaning out whatever suburban glut that brought you immense boredom."

"Don't fucking judge me," Mari said. "You met me an hour ago. I told you, I love your sister."

"You more than me," Kika said.

"I'd always asked her, and she couldn't answer me: How did it get to this? Where did it go so wrong for you?"

"Faulty genetics." Kika's tight lips curved, but it wasn't quite a smile. "*Leche de mala teta.* Faulty family lines and generational trees that uprooted and burned. Some of us are born unlucky. I guess you take pity on people like her and that's why you do what you do."

"Sure. It helps me forget all the other fucked-up shit in my life."

Kika gazed out at the street. "I take it there isn't much by way of police around here. I mean, you're supposed to call the cops to help find a missing person."

# CH. SIX

Jubilee had heard their boots grinding gravel. She knew exactly where she was. The smell of the bay. The stench of the landfill was a few miles away.

Billy spooned her inside the trunk, and they went for him first.

Familiar voices: men who'd crashed the party and their henchmen.

"What do we do with her?"

"Whatever the fuck you want."

# CH. SEVEN

They waited until dark before walking down toward the strip.

"So, what do you have planned?" Kika asked. "Other than feeling sorry for yourself?"

Mari stayed silent. At the end of the block, she said, "What are you thinking of doing?"

Kika said, "Let's get to know some of these faces."

"Ask around?"

"No. Too late for questions."

They made it to the pool hall, the sidewalk crowded with slummers and tourists. Kika listened to Mari drone on, absorbing every detail, even replaying the events in her mind. Across the street from the hall, they watched players leaning over billiard tables through the front window.

"The one with the blonde, spiky hair," Kika said. "Is that her?"

"Yeah. She was there. I saw her carry Jubilee out."

Kika pointed to a white sports car parked on the corner. "This the car they took you in?" she asked. "I can smell you've been in here. I can smell your blood in it."

Mari nodded and watched as Kika opened the car, tripped the alarm, and got in the backseat. Mari went in next to her and they waited. Kika was stiff and silent, almost as if she wasn't there. They watched everything from inside the car.

Embra split the rack. Sunk every one of them, over and over. An hour later, she collected from all the losers, mostly out-of-town frat boys pissed at losing to a woman. She stood out with her blonde, spiky hair, studded collar, tattoo sleeves, and beady eyes. Flexing biceps. Thick denim workpants, a leather vest over a white, collared shirt. With a mouth that could devour the world.

The voltage of her laughter crackled over the din of the pool hall. Something dry and sinister, a laugh declaring she could get away with anything. Blue eyes always scanning the room, always watching her Honey. Pushing away anyone who came near her Honey, the young woman with the gorgeous, pale face standing by the cue rack. With her big eyes and inviting lashes, candy-red lips, and a headful of curly hair that draped like one of Dolly Parton's old wigs. All Embra had to do was stare at her long enough and she'd float over to embrace her. When she arrived, Embra dipped her to the sound of shitty electro-pop-country from the jukebox, then brought her up and dove her face into her neck. Honey rode her thigh while yeehawing, holding steadily, pounding back shot after shot of whiskey. Whooping it up. Lips all over Embra's neck and face. Their wassail could be seen through the arched window, could be heard out in the street.

Outside the pool hall was as boisterous as inside, late-night crowds lining up around the block.

Kika climbed out and leaned against the small convertible, her neck and face damp from humidity. Hat hiding her face. Arms crossed. Her eyes never left the two women inside. Considered popping the hood and pissing on the battery but they would need the car.

Mari napped in the backseat, a hibernating ball of fear and depression.

Kika went around the car and tapped the glass to wake her. "Open up. They're coming."

In the dark, later, Kika said, "Are you crying?"

Mari wouldn't answer. She'd curled up tightly in the backseat. Kika sat beside her, knees pressed against her chest. Staring down at her. Deadpan eyes that said she was in total control.

"There were days where we slept in the attic just so we wouldn't hear our father beating our mother," Kika said. "Sometimes we slept in the car. We eventually abandoned our mother and he drove her to madness. Once, we ran away for a month, out in these streets. When we came back home, she was in the hospital a few days before she died from blunt trauma. So, slowly, I poisoned him. I didn't want him hurting my sister anymore. But when he died, he knew. And he told me he knew. They took us away and put us in a home. Upon further investigation, they determined it wouldn't be safe for them to release me. I don't recall exactly how many years I was locked away."

Mari opened her eyes. "Where will you two go once we find her?"

"I'm no longer concerned with running away. I'm just going to wait for the ground to open up and swallow me where I stand."

"You've got to take her as far from here as you can."

"Is there an out?" Kika asked. "What's done is done."

"You loved your mother a lot, and your sister," Mari said. "You were only protecting them."

"I only cared for our mother because I pitied her. I've never known the difference between love and pity. But I abandoned Jubilee."

"They took you from here," said Mari.

"No matter," Kika said. "There is something so terrible here in Carbon, something so viral that there is no cure and I want to see it burned to the ground."

# CH. EIGHT

"What's the hurry?" Embra asked.

They stumbled out of the pool hall, laughing. The night remained festive with Embra keeping the news of Phil's death to herself. Better to not fuck up a perfect night out with Honey. Let Blitz tell her. Or Reynolds. Tomorrow.

"I don't feel too good." Honey wobbled on high heels. She broke from Embra, who snatched her back by one of her skinny arms. Her hands were on her, everywhere.

Honey's accent was Floridian. Tropical southern. Whatever that was. Embra's was Carolina southern.

"All you had was a few sissy shots, big baby," Embra said.

"You drank the rest," said Honey. She wrapped both arms around Embra's neck. "No. I'm not letting you go. You can't ride drunk."

"No? You bringing my bike home? You think it's going to fit in the trunk of that midget car of ours?"

"We can come back for it tomorrow." Honey could barely get her words out with Embra smothering her face, pressing hard hands all over.

"Nah. Ride with me," Embra said.

"You don't have a helmet for me. And you're *fuuuucked* up."

"*Psst*, I drive better like this." Embra stood up straight, eyes closed, touching her nose, feigning a sobriety test. "I'm riding my bike home. And that's final. Don't follow too close." She kissed Honey hard and put a firm hand at her delta.

"Get home quickly," Honey said dizzily. "And in one piece!"

"You kidding?" said Embra. "I'm floatin' on angels' wings."

Giggling, Honey waved at her as she ducked into her tiny sports car that once belonged to Blitz. The fob didn't work so she used the key to unlock it. Ahead of the car, Embra mounted her neon-green crotch-rocket and ignited it. Behind the wheel, Honey struggled with the keys. Embra blew her a kiss, oblivious to the eyes peering out from the backseat, and peeled out.

*Rev, rev, zoom!*

Honey gripped the wheel and, Kika, her throat.

"You heard her. Don't follow too close." Kika's voice raised from the windy quarry of her soul, raspy and thick.

Honey sucked in a breath and Kika put her other hand over her mouth. She met her eyes in the rearview.

"Relax," said Kika. "Just drive. Follow her. Your girlfriend will be waiting for you." She sniffed Honey's ear and neck, inhaling Honey's skin, lips peeled back, close enough to eat her face. "You're not smelling so fresh, honey. Like you been drinking and smoking all night. Go on. Drive slowly."

Embra ran all the red lights, ripping into the night with an ear-splitting clamor.

"You want money?" Honey's voice cracked. "Take what you want." She reached for her purse.

Kika's dug her nails into her throat. "Ah-uh, honey. Both hands on the wheel. Don't take them off again."

Honey nodded. Her tears rolled and splashed Kika's hands.

"Your girlfriend was there when they took my sister from Billy Zombie's place," Kika said. "Were you there?"

Terrified, Honey shook her head. "No."

Kika squeezed harder.

"I don't hang out with my brother or his boys," Honey whispered. It was hard to swallow when Kika's hand could rip out her windpipe at any moment.

"Who's your brother?" Kika yanked her neck.

"Bobby… I mean B-Blitz."

"So, that cunt works with him. She knows where my sister is."

"I guess. How would I know? I don't even know your sister. They run everything. I'm just a girl. I don't get a say in the family business."

Kika to Mari: "You sure you saw that cunt there?"

"Yeah," Mari said. "She was there."

They followed the crotch-rocket down a winding two-lane road, into a new housing development. Townhouses no one could afford lining a figure-eight curve. Half-built domiciles, mounds of wood and concrete stacked at each lot. Every completed house was empty but one.

The front house lights came on as the garage door slowly opened. Embra revved the bike once more and skidded to a stop inside. The car hole was cluttered with half-built furniture, several-dozen boxes and wooden crates. She dizzily climbed off the crotch-rocket, pulling off her gloves and flexing her big hands. She looked out to the street and blinding high-beams when Honey's car took the curve and pulled up into the driveway.

"Turn those down, goddammit!" Embra shielded her face. Honey's silhouette approached and she was thrust onto her. Then a fist flew into Embra's face.

*Lights on.*

*Lights out.*

She fell hard on concrete.

The garage shut like the biting mouth of a primordial beast and the sound woke Embra. The overhead lamp buzzed and everything was blurry.

Kika kneeled on top of her. She'd left her hat in the car.

Embra opened one eye. Kika's fist closed the other.

Looked like the house expansion was coming together. There were brand-new tools hanging from the fiberboard walls, as well as several rolling tool cabinets. Heavy machinery. Backup generator. Beside the motorcycle sat a dozen neatly stacked crates, along with a standing band saw and compressor. Planks of wood. Packing straw. A giant glass bong, tall as a man.

"Use duct tape if you can't find a rope," Kika told Mari. Embra struggled under her, bold arms flexing and thrashing under Kika's stone-heavy knees. "Check those crates. Smash them open. Whatever it takes. Wreck the place."

Embra grunted. "There's…money inside. In my closet. I swear. You can take all of it."

"What's that gonna buy me?" Kika said. She leaned into her face, close enough to bite her nose off.

Mari cracked opened a crate with a long crowbar she grabbed from the wall of tools and then opened another crate.

"That one looks like a coffin," Kika said. "Check there."

Mari ran her hands through straw filling and looked back. "Guns. Lots of guns," she said.

"Any sign of my sister in there?" asked Kika.

"Uh. No?"

"Give me that."

Mari hesitated and then handed over the hooked, steel tool.

When Kika placed the bifurcated point in Embra's mouth and began impromptu dentistry, she had to look away.

# CH. NINE

Blitz didn't say hello when he barged into Seth's office, dumping himself on the vinyl loveseat in front of his desk. After a long and angry pause, Blitz said, "They slashed the Unholy Three! They shot Phil!"

"Funzo's on it." Seth looked at his desk phone, then noticed Blitz's bruised face.

"Yeah, I was with him." Blitz sizzled with manic energy. "He just dropped me off. He's pretty fucked up about it. But not like he's crying or anything."

"He's pissed he's got to clean up a lot of it. Don't worry. He's just lazy. Looks like he kissed you goodbye."

"I need a nurse."

"You let this happen."

"Fuck. No, I didn't," Blitz said. "Don't start with that shit. I don't party like that. We're in this together and cover our tracks when shit goes down. Always have. Why is everybody being a dick to me?"

"The Jamaicans are due this afternoon. Sure you didn't piss them off?"

"Nah, man. Reynolds is dealing with them. I haven't even talked to the buyers. That was between Phil and them. You know they won't let me in those meetings. We got the shit they ordered. They just have to come get it and pay us. Last of my worries."

"They're ass-deep in this," Seth said. "Trying to start a war."

"Fuck no," said Blitz. "Funzo's saying the same shit. But it can't be, man. We would've seen them creeping around. You sure they did this?"

"Busy weekend on the strip, Blitz. We can't know for certain. But most likely it was them. I mean, who else? Understand what I'm saying?"

"It's all hype for now." Blitz craned his neck and heard it crack. "I feel so blind. Don't you ever get out of your little cave here? I'm sure you feel all warm and cuddly with one of us always watching out for your ass."

Seth smirked. "Funzo's hyping the Jamaicans too."

"He's scared, putting on his tough-guy policeman act. He's shitting his pants 'cause he's losing control of everything."

"Right now, everything feels crazy," Seth said. "We got this trade happening, this business with Barry, and we gotta bid on a different waste management company."

"What?" Blitz said. "What happened with Palermo?"

"He'd rather stay in Miami Beach."

"Fuck him. Trash is just going to keep piling up in the streets. Before you know it, all of Carbon will be buried under it."

"Blitz, right now all I want is an inventory review. Double-check that everything is with Embra."

"If the Jamaicans move in with enforcers, there's not much we can do," Blitz said. "Okay. So, I'll go count guns, but I need Blanco to come with."

"He's staying with me," said Seth. "Reynolds is pooling a few out-of-town knock-arounds. He's in Florida with Abner and Miguelito. That leaves you with Embra right now. She hasn't called me back this morning."

"Why don't you come count with me?"

"Because that's not what I do. I have to stand in for Phil on the business front."

"Well, buddy, hate to break it to you, but this is the business."

"Have you called your sister?" Seth asked. "Maybe she can wake up Embra."

Blitz rolled his eyes.

"You got your toaster?" Seth asked.

"Toaster?" Blitz asked. "You mean my Glock? I kinda lost it last night. But whatever."

# CH. TEN

Looking down at the bloody pit of Embra's mouth and smiling, Kika said, "I'm just getting started."

Honey shrieked where she sat on a crate.

"Hit her," Kika said.

Mari slapped her.

"I said fucking hit her."

Mari punched her hard enough to crack a knuckle.

Honey reeled back, looking drugged and dazed. She cried into her hands.

"Get the fuck off!" Embra gargled blood and spat out teeth.

Kika smacked her with the flat end of the crowbar. "Tell me."

"Fuck off!"

"I need real answers, cunt." Kika shifted her knee to Embra's throat. Embra turned blue. Slowly, Kika moved off, standing over her. Her dress and arms were maroon with blood.

Mari stood behind her. "What did you do?"

"What do you think?" Kika said. She grabbed one of the rolling tool cabinets and pulled until it fell and crushed Embra under a cascade of tools and motorcycle parts. Embra's head tilted back, spitting one last spigot of blood. Kika grabbed a pair of pliers, teasing Embra's face before tucking them into her stockings.

Mari shook, fist curled into her breast.

Kika searched the garage, elbowing Mari out of the way. She rummaged the drawers of the other rolling toolbox, tossing papers and receipts aside, kicking at car parts, turning over crates. TEC-9s, Uzis, and saw dust fell at her feet. The propane torch hanging from a hook at the end of the table caught her eye. She pulled the hose until the tank rolled from under the table. She looked at Mari and smiled.

Mari's eyes lit up and she slowly backed away. Kika grabbed a wrench off the wall and slammed the tank valve until it hissed. Mari's eyes watered immediately. She masked her face with both hands. Honey coughed until she vomited. Kika breathed into her arm, fighting back nausea. She punched the garage door opener and immediately sucked in fresh air. Embra lay unconscious, unrecognizable under the tool cabinet.

Mari dragged Honey outside. Her face, arms, knees, and thighs were scraped and bloody. Pretty dress all mangled and soiled. Dazed, drooling, unaware.

Mari watched Kika by the garage door, igniting a greasy rag. "We need to drag her out!" Mari said, standing in front of the car.

Kika looked back at her. The rag ignited and flames ran up her arm. She tossed it into the gaseous garage and the gas caught.

As the house burned, Kika was overtaken in its gathering orange nimbus. She stood until smoke surrounded her, then slowly backed away, watching it all get consumed.

# CH. ELEVEN

"Wait," Funzo said.

Yumi, the skinny Thai hooker with an attitude, climbed out of his car.

He felt dazed in the kaleidoscope of her wardrobe: hot pink skirt, turquoise tank top under an orange fur wrap. Yellow platform shoes. Pink, furry purse.

"I'll give you a ride," he said.

"I'm just going to clean up and go back to work."

"I'll take you home. Sit up here with me."

# CH. TWELVE

"You take a shower first," Kika said after they stumbled into the motel room. The green and yellow ambiance made the place seedy and depressing. Dim lighting cast long shadows on the walls that became figures or faces. There were two beds, a desk, a chair, a set of drawers, and Kika's suitcase by the bathroom door.

"I... I still hear sirens," Mari said. She looked down at Honey curled on the floor, bound with bungee cords, a blindfold, and a gag.

Kika sat on the edge of her bed, removing blood-caked boots. "Let the motherfucker burn," Kika said, lying back on the flowered comforter. "And that bitch can stay on the floor."

"I can feel her pain." Mari sobbed. "This is cruel."

"My advice is to not feel anything. Ever. About anyone or anything."

"You feel anger all the time, don't you?"

"I'm running on instinct at this point," Kika said.

"Is eye-for-an-eye instinct?"

"Don't forget a tooth for a tooth." Kika scooped several of Embra's bloody teeth from her pocket and threw them at Mari.

"I mean, you feel love, right?" Mari said. "You came to get your sister out of Carbon."

Kika rolled over and ignored her.

Mari grabbed a towel from a small shelf and removed her shoes, left them by the door. Then she stood silently, rubbing her neck and shoulders. Checking her fingernails, the bruises on her hands and legs. The vomit and blood on her shirt and jeans. The streaks of dried mud and soot on her ankles and feet.

"I don't know if I can sleep with her just thrown there on the floor." Caressing her throat, Mari exhaled. Sweat pasted her short, black hair against her neck. Dark crescents swelled beneath her eyes. She was beginning to look like Kika.

"I don't have a problem with this bitch on the floor," Kika said. She rolled over and looked at Mari. "Watch how I do it. When my eyes close... I will be asleep."

"I haven't slept for weeks," Mari said.

"Same here. But you'll be surprised from where peace of mind arrives. Just shut your eyes and it'll come to you."

"Strange things happen whenever I wake up in strange motel rooms," Mari said.

"We're going to dangle her out there tomorrow as bait. Now's your last chance to sleep…or to run away. If she causes a ruckus, kick her face."

Mari went silently, closing the bathroom door behind her. When she came out, she wore a white robe. Steam followed her.

Kika was sleeping. Mari crawled into the other bed. All night long, she thought about the sobbing shape lying on the floor beside her. The gun she'd taken from Phil was still with her. Without revealing it to Kika, she tucked it under her pillow. She rested her head directly on top of it and cried. She sobbed quietly for a long time before reaching for it and placing it at her head.

Then she put it back, hand curled around it. It felt cold but flaccid. She could never fire it again.

Holding it didn't make her feel any safer.

# CH. THIRTEEN

"I really don't want to stick around," Blitz told Seth.

"What, leave Carbon? Fly out with Barry? That son of a bitch won't even let you touch a single propeller, much less board his precious plane. He told me in private that you're just bad luck. No, really. This is a true story. I'm not superstitious, but it's his plane. And don't let Reynolds hear you say you don't want to stick around."

"I just wanna leave for a while. This is too much to handle right now."

"Just when this shit is lighting up? You really want to feel the wrath of Reynolds, don't you? Everybody will know you went to Atlanta. They'll find you even faster. Maybe send someone after you. Reynolds still needs you as a liaison. Because you're blood. Come on, man. You're a big boy now. Time to show that you can handle big business. For the sake of your brother, take this business seriously."

"That's all bullshit," Blitz said. "Phil didn't know what the fuck was happening any more than I did. He was just the oldest brother and talked better."

"You don't seem affected by what happened to him," Seth said. "Focus."

"You too with this shit? I've had a rough couple of days, man."

"You had it rough? What, seeing how much blow and ass you could bury your face in? Tell that to Philip. I think they're still looking for the right side of his face. How about Billy Zombie. Did Funzo clear that up?"

"Blanco and a few others cleaned it up."

"When it's your time, are you going to be able to sign on the dotted line?"

"What?"

"Metaphorically speaking."

"Man, this is why I hate talking to you," Blitz said. "You use big terminology. It's going to be a quick exchange, some handshakes, and all smiles. Done."

"You're delusional, man," Seth said. "This ain't fucking trading cards. If that was a preemptive strike, they've already made up their minds how it's going down."

"If that's how you look at it... I say if they wanna war, let them roll in and we take them out during the trade. On our turf. We turn those guns against them. Problem solved."

Seth drummed his fingers on some paperwork. "Take into consideration what it may set off. If you're set on this, and I know you're no strategist, at least have the smarts to build a parameter. Go get the crates and relocate them. I got a lot of calls to make right now."

# CH. FOURTEEN

Mari woke to the moist sound of Kika masturbating.

Kika's back was pressed hard against the mattress, knees bent, right hand blurred in motion against her exposed pubis.

Mari waited until she finished, watching her come down with a low moan, settling back onto the bed.

Kika ignored her, pulled down her dress and walked to the bathroom. Mari waited for the sounds of her urinating before she got up. The faucet ran and then Kika came out, drying her hands. They hovered over Honey's odd position: her back arched, head twisted, face blue, and vomit oozing from her nostrils.

"What now?" Mari said, holding her throat. For a brief time in her abyssal sleep, she'd forgotten all about Honey.

Kika looked down, but her eyes drifted. "We gotta go. Leave her here. Take her car, trade it for something else."

"Wait! No," Mari said. "This has to fucking stop. I'm not touching her."

"No one said you had to," said Kika. "Leave her. Ever notice how this town is just one giant landfill? Ever since I can remember, people were always dying around me."

Mari went to grab her soiled clothes off the bed, but instead went for the gun under the pillow.

Kika swung against the motion of Mari's loaded arm and clawed her throat. She pushed her down on top of Honey on the floor.

"Everything happens fast." Kika pressed her foot into her gun hand until it loosened. "Everything accelerates the closer you are to death."

Tearful and fear-filled, Mari said, "Okay... I'm sorry. Please. That hurts."

Kika stepped harder.

Mari saw her grin and heard her growling. "I didn't mean it," Mari said. "I'm just scared. You... You're acting crazy. I'm starting to understand how what you've been through made you like... *this*."

"Made me what?" Kika said. "Fucking say it: made me crazy? Is that what you're telling me?" She grabbed Mari and threw her around the room.

Mari rolled and grabbed the gun, putting it into Kika's belly.

"Yeah." Kika smiled. "Do it. Do us both a favor and pull it." She grabbed her arm and placed the gun under her chin. "I wanna kick open the doors of Hell and tell them I'm coming."

"What the fuck do we use for collateral now?" Mari yelled. "We'll never get to Jubilee. We've lost. All of it. What now?"

"Use this fucking thing or get it out of my face. Next time you aim it, you better fucking mean it." Kika pushed her against the wall and went to her suitcase for fresh clothes.

# CH. FIFTEEN

"It's just you and your family out here in the projects?" Funzo drove her home.

Yumi sat as far from him as she could, hands clenched between her thighs. Her knees were scraped and scabbed. Blood-streaks oozed down her legs, into her boots. "No. Just me. My family lives in Pennsylvania. I'm on the other side of the landfill, in Cordial."

"This is the shortcut," Funzo said.

"Um, okay."

His eyes were on her more than the road. "Did you come down here to make movies?" Funzo asked. "Pornos?"

"Not at first," she said. "Carbon had better clubs back then."

"How old are you?"

"19. Are you arresting me?"

"Are you wearing handcuffs right now?" Funzo said. "Why didn't you stay in the car with those boys?"

"I was scared," she said.

"Of Blitz?"

"All of them. They actually kicked me out into the street."

"Philip is dead, you know," said Funzo.

"Oh… I heard that. Shit. Who did it?"

"It's best if you don't know."

"Can I smoke in your car?"

"Cigarette?" he said.

"Just a cigarette," Yumi said.

"I don't want you stinking up the car. Open the window."

Yumi lit up, sucked in hard, held it. The cigarette was breakfast.

"You remember around what time that was? Where'd you go?" Funzo asked, eyes searching her open purse.

She blew smoke out of the window as hard as she could. "Can't remember. We were at the bar and then the car. We stopped to pick up some rubbers. The car didn't stop until they tossed me out on the street. Fucking assholes."

He chuckled. "Next time, wear kneepads."

Her pout turned into a comical duck face.

"I can see you're the little girl who lost her way," Funzo said. "Think there's a chance?"

"What's that supposed to mean?" she asked.

"This is a shit town. God, it fucking stinks."

"We're driving through a landfill, duh. You're always here. I see you patrolling up and down this road all the time."

"There's a lot of business I take care of out here," he said. "What you don't see won't hurt you, am I right?"

She gave him a nervous, uncomfortable look. "I guess."

"And you're sure Blitz wasn't there with you and them boys? He wasn't in the car with you?"

"No, we just did shots at the bar with him," she said. "I would have remembered if he'd fucked me. His cock looks like a hairy potato. It was just the three other guys. Why, you think he set them up? I already talked to the other cops about it."

"But you never came back home last night," Funzo said.

"I didn't feel like walking back," Yumi said. "I slept on a bus bench until sunrise. I woke up and Blitz was there like he'd been tweaking all night. A patrol car stopped by and asked some questions. Blitz was too fucked up to answer anything."

"Uh-huh," Funzo said.

"My house is just over there. Can I get out here? I'll just climb the trash hill and go through the hole in the fence."

"And you didn't see anybody else? Anybody who looked out of place, anybody you'd never seen in Carbon before? Like black guys with dreadlocks."

"It was Sunday. The strip is always asleep on Sundays. You know, liquor laws and shit. I would have remembered islanders if I saw them. They do shit like this?"

"Shit like what?" said Funzo.

"Like this gangster shit."

"Who said anything about gangsters?"

"Well…" Yumi said. "You asked me about Blitz and his boys."

"Those boys, they were a bunch of assholes. What'd they ever do to deserve that?"

"I can give you a list."

"Oh yeah? You keep a list? You write this stuff down?"

"No, I mean I can tell you some shit. They were my best customers."

Funzo grinned. "I see you got some shit calculating up there, under that cute wig."

"I'm not a narc," she said. "You gonna let me off here?"

"How's life on Garbage Island?"

"It stinks. That's for sure. Ha-ha. I just come home to shower and change costumes. I practically live on the strip."

The car abruptly stopped.

She flicked her cigarette out the window and got out. She slammed the door, walking parallel as he drove beside her.

"I want to make sure you know," Funzo said.

She stopped to look inside the passenger window. "What?"

Funzo waited for her to lean into the car, then shot her in the throat and chest.

Rendered faceless, her legs gave under her.

He looked over the passenger door to see her lying in brush covered with shredded papers and cigarette butts. Part of an old bus stop bench grew out of the sedges.

He parked and inspected her body. Her face had imploded. He looked around, took a breath, grabbed her heels, and dragged her toward a pile of roadside trash. She'd be found a lot faster this way and he wanted to leave her to the archeologists. Singlehandedly by one heel, he dragged her back to the car while fumbling with his keys in the other hand.

The dead traveled faster. She was a hundred pounds or less. Her boots were heavy toasters on tiny feet. He opened the trunk to a swarm of angry flies. They crawled and gathered around his mouth and went up his nose. A few made a permanent home above his eyebrow. He cursed and swatted as he placed her body among the cargo and closed the trunk.

He couldn't remember the last time he'd seen the landfill gate locked. The Humps, they called it. Pyramids of garbage overlooking a landscape dotted by more mounds of trash and the occasional hobo shack. He cursed his way to the gate, unlocked it, and got back behind the wheel. He rode in, smoking a crumbled cigarette he'd found in her purse. He'd taken her cash too, a pair of her thong panties, and her lipstick. He drove deep into a wasteland of refuse and debris. When he found a place to park, he lifted her out of the trunk and dragged her over the quaggy terrain. Her head hit a car fender protruding from the brittle dirt, knocking her wig off. The uneven ground shifted beneath his weight. The further he went, the softer the soil was. He waddled quickly to not lose footing. When he found solid ground, he let her go. Tapping his foot in a circle, he reached out and punched the ground. After some digging and struggling, out came a shovel. He plunged the earth with it and dug. The air stunk. The earth was stinking, he was stinking.

She'd been unplanned but was at the right place, right time. With little fanfare, he rolled her into the shallow excavation, went back for her wig, and threw it at her face. He kicked toxic dirt and garbage on top of her until she was interred. He slammed the shovel over the mound he formed, then stomped it a few times. He added newspapers, more dirt. Once completed, he walked backward, crossing himself. The ground was too soft to hold him, and he tumbled into an old excavation. A plump, bluish hand flopped sideways out of the ground, maggot-gnawed and rotting. Lying in the shallow grave, he punched the hand until it interred. The more he struggled, the more he sank into the hugging arms of the corpse. He clawed his way out on his hands and knees, then got to his feet, wiping his hands. He scooped dirt with his shoe over the fissure until it was a grave again.

"God." He crossed himself and spat, fighting back nausea. With a grimace, he searched the perimeter, counting the places where the earth had been recently turned. The mounds. Graves. He counted the marking posts. Signs only he could interpret. Coffee cans. Milk crates. The shell of a hair dryer. Old tires. These were the places. Garbage ornaments marking all the graves. More than two dozen. In this quadrant, anyway.

His phone rang in his pocket. He choked and gasped and coughed.

"Seth," he said, clearing his throat.

"Just got off the phone with them. Would have been easier to send a smoke signal. Location's changed."

"For the exchange?"

"Exactly."

"I figured as much," Funzo said. He loosened his tie and wiped his forehead with it.

"Reynolds is en route," said Seth. "Could be end of day, by the time he gets back. He'll miss lunch at least."

"You with Blanco?"

"Yeah. He's not the brightest though. They could have given me someone, um, more conversational."

"Hey, he came out the gutter and cleaned up. Cut him a fucking break. He can't hear too well, on account of his last fight. He's still at it, failed boxing career and all. You gotta give him that. He's good muscle. Doesn't mean he's a dunce. He's got ADD. Be good to him."

"He's a good lapdog." Seth chuckled.

"That's what you have to do with these grease-monkeys. He's been doing great since you promoted him to bodyguard. Don't be afraid to sic him at the other dogs. He'll fuck 'em up."

"It looks like his best years might be behind him. They said that about you too."

Funzo grunted. "I'm a long way from retiring, buster. Your fucking humor may have worked on Phil or maybe Blitz, but it won't work on me. That's why I'm still alive, motherfucker. Pay attention to dinosaurs. Watch them closely. They'll tell you a lot about history, so you don't have to fuck up and repeat their mistakes."

"I'm kidding, asshole," Seth said. "Where the fuck are you?"

"Don't worry about it and I don't have time for your shit so shut the fuck up."

"What are you doing?"

"Cleaning up messes. This badge ain't no good anymore. Should've been a garbage man instead."

# CH. SIXTEEN

Location: Middleburg.

On the next block was the old cigar factory, now just a cavernous warehouse-turned-boxing gym. American and Korean flags hand-painted across the zinc doors. On a wooden placard over the door was the inscription **Mario's Box**.

Reynolds and Miguelito led the expedition.

Music echoed from inside. A barefoot kid, about 26, walked out to meet them, holding a vintage boom box about the size of a beer cooler, blasting music from the rap group Brooklyn Academy. The kid was about 5'8", wearing raggedy cutoffs and a stained tank top. He had a head of messy curls and thick glasses. He got straight to the point: "Yo, I heard about your boy Phil," he shouted. "My deepest condolences."

Reynolds looked at Miguelito. "News travels," he said. "Hey, can you turn that down?"

"Oh yeah, yeah. Listen, it's a pleasure working with you guys. I mean I feel so honored and all, working with a couple of made guys—"

"Whoa, whoa, bro," Miguelito said. He was a short man, late twenties. Blotchy, patchy brown skin, feathered hair, collared shirt, and jeans. Mustache looked more a suggestion than growth. "Slow yo' roll. Nobody's made nobody. We're not talking about any of that right now. And we're not working with you."

"Yous guys work for Mr. Phil, right?"

"That's right," Reynolds said. "You the guys from New York?"

"Nah," said the kid. "I'm from Trenton, Jersey."

"Slow down," Miguelito said. "You talk too fast. We came looking for Chong. I thought you was professionals. What happened to this place?"

"Oh yes, sir. Absolutely. I am a professional. We're pros, bro, we're pros. Mos def."

"How come you're barefooted, my man?"

"It's how I roll. You know 'cause we do karate." The kid pronounced it *kah-raw-tee*. "You know, don't wanna be kicking nobody with soft feet, na'mean? Be kicking somebody and then be like, 'Aw, damn, my foot!' Na'mean?"

"Sure, man," Miguelito said. "Is Chong here?"

"Ain't no Chong here, my guy. That's Chino to you, bro. And he can't see nobody 'til I approve it. I'm the gatekeeper here."

"Listen," Reynolds started. "We drove all morning and then waited out here an hour because your guy didn't want to get up early to meet us. There's plenty of other people we can get for this work."

The kid took a second look at them. He smiled uneasily. His eyes looked tiny behind his thick glasses. "All right, all right," he said. "He and me, we go way back. You know how I met Chino?"

"No, haven't heard this one," Reynolds said. His arms bulged when he crossed them.

"I was at a karate demo, right?" the kid said. "Wasn't regular karate, it was Christian Karate. Is like instead of meditating, we pray to God, praise Jesus. Uh-huh. Praise the Lord. We pray before we get things started. Back then we used to demo at malls and shit. State fairs, churches, shit like that. After one of our mall demos, I hooked up with a couple of the tae-kwan-do dudes and we went down to this place called McDuff's Smorgasbord. This was down near Richfield Park, you know, 'cause you can't have shit like that in Trenton. Man, used to be the best place to get stuffed. All the roast beef you could ever care to eat, my man, $7. It was right across the street from the mall. We was all starving, having been at demos all day and shit.

"So, we walk in, wearing our karate suits and right away get hassled by a bunch of hillbillies from Elizabeth or some fucking place outside our turf. One altercation led to another, next thing you know, we're in the parking lot, tightening up our belts, cracking our knuckles, doing stretches. We're like, 'Aw shit, they outnumber us!' And soon enough, Chino come around, dressed in his red gi and he's like, 'You rednecks get back or I'm ah fuck ya up!' The head hillbilly got pissed off, so he pulled out a gun and then Chino spin-kicked him and busted all his teeth out. One fucking kick! Hillbilly got on his knees, talking 'bout, 'You busted my teeth, you spic mothafucka!' He said he'd be running home to get his cousin and bring more guns, but I never saw that motherfucker again. Shit, my man Chino... He's a fucking truck, bro. I promise you won't be disappointed. I owe him my life. That's why I hang out here, cleaning up, bringing girls by. That kind of shit. What I'm trying to say is dis man got yo' back, son. How 'bout it? Did he pass the audition?"

"That's a great piece of history," Reynolds said. "What was your name?"

"I'm Garcia, bro." He stuck up a hand to slap but was left hanging.

Reynolds was a hand-shaker. "Garcia," he said. "Can we meet Chino now?"

"Sure, my man. Gimme like fifteen. He's getting dressed. He was heading out to score some knuckle, if you know what I mean."

"I don't," Miguelito said.

"He got your call and canceled," Garcia said. He had them follow him into the warehouse. He started up the boom box then went into an office. They waited a few minutes and, finally, Chino appeared. The overhead lamp was dim, but he lit the room with energy. There was a succession of board breaking and brick cracking. He went through his kata demonstration and motions before saying anything. He was medium height, a thick Puerto Rican with Asiatic eyes, with a helmet of feathered hair. He had on stretch-jeans that allowed kicks over his head, a tight, orange T-shirt with a tiger iron-on and his name stitched across the back. He spun, thrust fists, chopped, and kicked. Broke furniture, kicked gravel bags, all while Garcia blasted Stevie B's "Party Your Body" from his boom box. Chino posed and demoed all over blue Century floor mats, letting out several sharp "Ki-*ya*"s.

"Where's his karate suit?" Miguelito asked.

"It's called a gi, bro," Garcia said. "He don't need it. He don't believe in uniforms. He don't fuck with conformity."

Chino walked to the wooden dummy at the corner of the mat and did a few rounds with it. "I'm representing me," he said with a high lisp. "I don't need no jacket to say rank or what I am."

Again, Miguelito shot a sideways glance at Reynolds. Miguelito could sense his boredom three feet away.

Garcia flipped the tape in the boom box, and Chino continued his presentation. He finished beating the wooden dummy, worked on the worn-out punching bags again, stopped, bowed, and walked towards them. He signaled Garcia to kill the beats. "If you want me to take on Jamaicans, it's gonna cost you extra." Chino stopped in front of Reynolds and threw a roundhouse kick that came within inches of hitting him.

"Hey!" Reynolds ducked left. "What the fuck?"

Chino posed, sweated, moved to his own beat. Tilted his head side to side, cracking his neck, jogging in place, throwing air punches.

"Chill." Miguelito chuckled. "We haven't even named a price. If you're right off the street, you're at standard pricing, my man. It's what we pay all the young, fresh crew men."

"And who the fuck said anything about Jamaicans?" Reynolds asked.

"It's obvious, man," Chino said. "People been whispering shit. Say they're coming to take over. I just want to be on the side that's winning. And $500 ain't gonna cover it, is all I'm saying."

"I don't know," Reynolds said. "Gotta take it up with the chief. This is just a defense line we're building now. There's no war starting up or nothing. This is a preparation. Just in case. Got me?"

"Not how I hear it, boss." Chino stepped close. Garcia watched them volley from the sidelines. "Word is you're in charge now that Phil is gone. Was it them who took him out?"

"Can't say for certain," Reynolds said.

"C'mon, man, there's no way it wasn't. It's obvious. They're just starting a slow decimation. One by one. S'how they do it. I can't argue with what you got planned. Getting the troops in place just in case. I say, knife 'em where and when you can. Get 'em first, when they least expect it. I'll stick my neck out, but it's gonna be more than $500. And my partner here comes too."

"What's he gonna do?" asked Miguelito.

"Wind him up, let him go. You just wait and see what my man Garcia can do."

"All right," Reynolds said. "I'll give him half of what I give the others. No negotiating. He can stand in and make it look like we got more troops than there are." Reynolds put his hands at his waist. "You got five minutes to get your shit together and get to the car."

"Yeah, man," Miguelito chortled. "Put on your little ballerina shoes. You're going dancing."

"Yo, these are my kung-fu shoes." Chino snapped his fingers. Garcia rushed to a locker against the wall and brought back a towel to drape around Chino's neck.

"All right," Reynolds said. "When the time comes, I hope your ballet skills will be able to toss those motherfuckers like we need you to. Take a shower. You ain't stinking up my car."

# CH. SEVENTEEN

It was one of those new Cadillacs that looked like a sports car. Two doors. Seth was driving. Blanco sat in the backseat, mumbling to himself.

"Roomy," Blitz said from the passenger side. "I like this shit. I was telling Phil to get one. It's like a fucking spaceship. Goddamn, it's so fucking foggy out here."

"Where's your new ride?" Seth asked.

"Left it parked in front of the club. It got fucked in the fire."

"You parked it where I told you never to park it."

"Yep. It always kept people from stealing the rims though."

"And now it's burnt," said Seth.

"Yep. The tires on the right side all melted."

"Did you file your claim?"

"Not yet." Blitz yawned.

"Come on, man. It's not going to pay for itself like that."

"Don't worry about it. I got it covered."

Seth checked his teeth in the rearview and straightened his tie. He eyeballed Blanco like checking on a child. "Billy Zombie had to have been in on it," Seth said. "Who does he know that can do that kind of damage?"

"Everybody knows Billy," Blitz said. "From here, and up and down the Florida coast, Atlanta, Rome, Birmingham. But he wouldn't do shit like this. He'd have been too fucked up to try it. Carbon may be a toilet but he knew not to shit in it. Nobody he ran with could pull that. Not even those druggie hipster kids. I call bullshit on that theory. That's the stupidest thing I've heard all week. Had to be outsiders."

"Gotta cover all ground," Seth said. "Every possibility. It's a small fucking town. I mean, come on."

"And the Jamaicans couldn't have done it?"

"Why? They just want guns. That was the deal. This isn't about territory. I don't know those people and they have their own turf. They wouldn't fuck with us if they need us to sell them guns."

Blitz scratched the scruff on his neck. "We could talk about this all day but they're really the only ones that are even remotely aware of what we got here."

"But, really. Could Billy have been in with them?"

"I don't know. Maybe. He hung out with hippies that pretend to be Rastas. Maybe that's the connection."

"White Rastas?"

"Maybe they were the ones he was going to sell to, but he got stupid," Blitz said. "Maybe this was done on his behalf. Maybe they're coming for our stock and his drugs because he sold us out."

Seth adjusted his grip on the steering wheel. Blitz seen him perspire. Pit stains.

"He was some stupid kid, bragging and showing off in front everybody," Blitz said. "Billy fucked around and ignored Phil. And that's that. There's no way he organized anybody to retaliate."

"Who was at Billy's that night?"

"A bunch of fucking hipsters from around town," said Blitz. "Most of them cleared out by the time we got there. We even did some lines with them before taking them out."

"Took them out?" Seth asked.

"They threw Billy and a few girls in the trunk. I'd split by then."

"And Phil?"

"He went with Blanco and Reynolds, maybe Miguelito too, I guess."

"Yeah," Blanco said from the back. "I didn't see nothing."

"Any other stragglers?" asked Seth. "Anybody that you burned on a deal?"

"Stranglers?" Blanco asked.

"Buddy, I'm talking to Blitz. You burn anybody recently, B? Anybody with a vendetta coming for Phil or you?"

"How the fuck should I know?" Blitz asked. "With the kind of shit we deal with, you're liable to catch a bad break and get a knife in your eye at any given time."

"It was a bullet," Seth said.

"Whatever, man. Everybody's coming at me with questions, and I don't know shit. You guys keep me in the shadows and, well, I don't see shit, I don't know shit."

"Could be that you're just never around. Everybody thinks you're still that pill-pusher kid from high school. Reynolds is moving up and you're right below. What's your strategy?"

"Number one: fuck off," Blitz said. "I'm tired of hearing it, man. Fucking sick of it. And what about you? You're not going to try to take a piece of it?"

"I'm just the company lawyer, man. Money-transfer man, if you will. Document signer. Notary public. Call me when you need to make a court appearance. I'm on retainer, either way."

"I'm not doing this shit by myself, Seth. Are we putting the shit in your trunk?"

"We're not picking this up yet. You're going to wait at the club and sit tight for Reynolds to return with a crew."

"The club's burnt to the ground."

"Well, stand out front, stick a toothpick in your mouth, pretend you're James Dean. I don't give a shit. Just stand there and wait. Call Embra and tell her you'll be there by noon."

"Do you know the guys riding with Reynolds?" Blitz asked.

"New recruits from Florida," Seth said. "Jacksonville area."

"Jacksonville? Nigger and wetback laborers, probably."

"Herd's been thinning out. You know, jail. And death."

"Shit, my boys would've handled this shit."

"Your boys are fucking dead," Seth said. "You got any better ideas? This was all last minute. Babysit this shit and stand by."

The car stopped.

"I should be at this meeting with you," Blitz said. "Instead, I'm gonna spend the day hauling crates. Is this my first day or something? My club burned to the ground. How much more am I going to be punished?"

Seth snapped his fingers at him. "See, there you go. You're telling me what you can't do. Why is that, Blitz? Are you not part of this team or do you just show up when it's convenient? You don't like the setup, talk to Reynolds when he gets back."

"Bro. I've never once seen you move any of this shit around. Never seen you at the warehouse, lifting or hauling anything or going down to Florida to bring back contraband."

"That's because it's not my fucking job," said Seth. "You think you can go to this meeting with the Jamaicans and carry the money back? Now, get out and wait."

Blitz looked at Blanco.

The ex-boxer in the backseat looked up and stuck out his tongue.

"Later," Blitz said and stepped onto the sidewalk.

# CH. EIGHTEEN

The valley of trash was dense with smog. The air smelled of chemical fires and the sweet sourness of trash. The car stalled several dozen yards from the gate, where the smog was dense as concrete. Two figures emerged, dragging something behind them. They'd run out of fuel. Now they walked the rest of the way, dragging Blitz.

"There's a whole gang of them," Mari said. "There's only two of us."

"It gets easier," said Kika, chewing gum and pulling Blitz by the neck with the hook-end of the crowbar. "They'll see two women walking alongside the road and their response will be to whip their dicks out the window at us. That's when we cut them off."

Mari just nodded her head.

"Do you believe in God?" Kika asked.

Mari's response was immediate. "Not really."

"Going forward, believe in a god of wrath, a god whose face is a mass of entrails, whose breath smells of excrement, who rules over plagues... Then you will feel this power and you will fear nothing. Most certainly, you will fear no man."

Mari's mouth was a thin, pale line. She said, "I think the vultures are following us."

Kika grinned toward the sky. "And crows. Don't forget the crows. This town's built on top of several generations of trash. It's collapsing under its own weight. When it burns so bright, they'll see the fire from the moon."

They pierced the smog's nebulous curtain, walking across the landfill. They breathed the gaseous, restless singularity of a thousand ghosts trapped in this toxic, littered landscape.

# CH. NINETEEN

The mint-green 1977 Thunderbird was parked in front of the gym. A small mulatto man with a face like a frog waited behind the wheel. He wasn't so much a little man as he was a stunted man. With a complex.

"The boys all upgraded," Miguelito said to Reynolds. Garcia and Chino walked behind them toward the car. "I mean, that Thunderbird's a classic and I appreciate that you kick it old school, but that lawyer got a brand-new sports Caddy."

"Yeah, fuck all that," Reynolds said. "His daddy bought him the Caddy. This beast belonged to my uncle. I can drive it through a fucking wall like a tank."

"Seats are kinda hard and cold, boss."

"Where's your ride, Richard Petty?"

"Had to give it to my girl," Miguelito said.

"If she's not riding your face back and forth, is she even your girlfriend?"

"Nah, boss, I didn't mean—"

"That T-bird's been with me a long time," Reynolds said. "And it's staying with me until its last gasp."

"Yo, my Toyota's on the other block," Garcia said, leaning to one side from the weight of his massive boom box.

"We all get in one car," Reynolds commanded. "This one. Get in. This here's Little Abner at the wheel."

Garcia was climbing in when Miguelito stopped him. "Hold up, son. Where the fuck you putting that thing?"

"My lap, bro," Garcia said.

"Nah, man. Put it in the trunk. Ab, pop her open."

Packed three in the back and Reynolds in the passenger seat, Abner focused on the highway, both hands on the wheel, foot heavy on the gas pedal. Sometimes slowing down for the speed limit, but mostly breaking it.

"Blanco just texted me," Miguelito said, begrudgingly sitting next to Chino. "They're on their way to intercept."

"I'm surprised he knows how to use a phone," Reynolds said. He looked back at Miguelito. "We'll be short a man with Phil gone."

"Fucking shame what happened," Garcia said. "When's the funeral?"

"Relax, bro," Miguelito said. "Body's still warm."

"Family will be coming in from out of town," Reynolds said. "There'll be all the usual bullshit. But first we got business to settle, find out why they burned down the fucking club when all they wanted was guns."

"They gonna have a party after the funeral?" Garcia asked. "Like food and shit?"

"Yeah," said Reynolds. "But the family may object to you grease-monkeys being invited."

Garcia lowered his eyes. "I know, boss."

"Call me Reynolds."

"Right, right," said Garcia. "We're here to do the dirty work. I wish him and his family my best. He'll be vindicated. That's why we're here. God bless."

"I'll fix you guys up each with a piece when we get there." Miguelito lit a cigarette, blowing smoke out the back window.

"Don't need them," Chino said. "I got foot and fist."

"That's right," Garcia said. "This motherfucker can catch bullets between his teeth. I, myself? I wouldn't mind an AK or something more than a peashooter."

"That's our stock and trade," said Miguelito. "You ever shot an automatic weapon?"

"Nah, not really," Garcia said. "But I'm looking to expand my network of tactics."

"Listen to this guy." Miguelito laughed.

Garcia withdrew. "What?"

"Stop talking out of your ass, man," Chino told him.

Garcia cleared his throat and remained quiet for several miles. Then he said, "So, as I understand, it was the Jamaicans moving in? We going to war with the Jamaicans?"

"We already told you…" Miguelito lit another cigarette.

"They coming to Carbon?" Chino asked. With his face aimed at the sun, he looked like a 70s magazine icon: feathered hair, dimples, exposed shoulders.

"That town's growing, bro," Garcia said. "I mean, it's close to the beach. Reminds me of the Jersey Shore."

They vacillated and mumbled. Reynolds looked at Abner.

"You believe this?" Reynolds asked. "I got a carload of brown 'cause I figured you spics would all get along if I hired you."

"Ain't a spic," Chino said. "I'm Italian."

"No, you ain't, motherfucker." Garcia laughed. "Your sister may sport a mustache, but that bitch is Puerto Rican!"

"How about you, mulatto?" Chino tapped Abner.

"Dominican, bro." Abner kept his eyes on the road.

"Did you get that overbite from sucking dick?" Chino asked. That cracked Miguelito up.

"Hey, hey," Reynolds cut in. "You don't know these boys like that. Watch yourself. Else you find your ass on the side of the road, hitchhiking back."

"You know what, *pendejo?*" Abner told Chino. "When we get done, it's you and me, man. Fuck's wrong with you, disrespecting me like that?"

"Let's do it now, bitch," Chino said. "Pull over."

"No, goddamn it!" Reynolds said. "The both of you shut the fuck up. I know you all got it bottled up in you. Wait. Just fucking wait. Save that shit for the Jamaicans."

They managed several more miles in silence until Garcia said, "How about you, Reynolds? What are you? You ain't no spic."

"He's a fucking Polack," Miguelito said, laughing like it was his first time trying out the word.

"Yeah, fuck you too, wetback." Reynolds flipped him off.

"Yo," Abner said. "That's what they call Mexicans. I'm not Mexican."

"Brown is brown, L'il Abner," said Reynolds.

"Ain't nothing wrong with Mexicans," Garcia said. "They're just like human mules. But they get shit done. And I love tacos."

"Good help is hard to find," Reynolds humored him.

"Yeah, but they ruined Spanish," Garcia said. "Ever talk to a Mexican? I can't understand a single thing they say."

"Man, you don't even speak Spanish." Chino elbowed him.

"Yeah, I do. A little, at least. I can't understand their dialect. They just make up their own shit."

"They ain't worse than Puerto Ricans," said Abner.

Chino stared at the back of his head and whispered, "But nothing's worse than a fucking Dominican."

"What was that, Ponch?" Abner said. "Yeah. That's what I thought."

"I went to a Chinese place two weeks ago," Garcia started. "Mexicans ran the place. Can't complain. Food was awesome."

"They run everything," Reynolds told them with a managerial tone.

"Next time we should get a crew of wetbacks to do all this dirty work," said Miguelito.

"Why?" Reynolds asked. "I got all the spics I need here. I'm not saying I won't bring Mexicans on board, though. We don't discriminate. Right? Why don't you lead that campaign, Miguelito?"

"I was just sayin', boss…"

Reynolds looked hard at him. "You're saying a lot of shit. All of you, just keep quiet. I'm trying to figure this shit out."

# CH. TWENTY

Bruised, they shared a bent cigarette. The sheet of ice between them was thick enough to skate on. Mari checked herself in the sun visor's mirror. She'd used makeup from Honey's purse to cover up scratches and bruises on her face and neck. Because of the difference in complexions, it wasn't the best disguise.

Kika drove.

"Please don't mention again how this isn't how you wanted it to go," Kika said. Whenever she spoke, it came from another place, a distant plane: atop a mountain or from the abyss of a black cave. "Once you kill, you condemn yourself to solitude."

"I feel guilty," said Mari. "And paranoid. We have to get rid of this car."

The service road widened and, suddenly, they were cruising on a four-lane strip that cut through the town.

"When we're done, we can drive it into Carcass Bay," Kika said.

"They're going to kill us."

"Let 'em come. The human animal finds a truer meaning of existence when put in extreme situations. We're not here to win them over. We'll finish this."

Mari tensed up. She kept turning around, looking behind them. There were very few cars on the street today.

"Who said that?" Mari asked.

"I don't know," said Kika. "I paraphrase. Didn't you read something like that in school?"

Back window, side window. Forward.

"When did you arrive in Carbon?" Mari asked. "How many days have you been here?"

"I don't remember," said Kika. "Memory is dull. But I entered town right about that street there. Stumbled out of the dark as I was passing by. Thought I'd wrench my sister away from here."

"Passing by? How'd you get here? Greyhound bus?"

Kika shrugged. "No. I was on my way to treatment. To the place where they frequently burned my brain in order to cure it. Poisoned me with so many prescriptions that memories are patchy at best. Nothing is true."

"What was the cure for?" Mari asked.

"Lucidity. They liked to keep me in a haze. But I see a lot better without their 'medicine.' They wanted to shape and control my reality. They called me crazy. I wanted... I wanted to take Jubilee out of here, once and for all. They couldn't find a cure for me, but they can at least try it with her."

"I don't think any shock treatment can help her," Mari said. "She won't leave with you, I'm sure of that. If I couldn't get her cleaned up, certainly you…"

"Even if have to kill her, I *will* put her out of her misery."

"Have mercy on her. She's your flesh and blood." Mari looked at the Bible Kika had put on the dashboard after leaving the motel. "It says so in your holy book."

"It's not my book," said Kika. "And there's nothing holy about it. If anything, it's a guidebook for lunatics, the blueprint for the shit of God. After you commit yourself to the treatment, you also have to submit to their god to prove your worthiness. You know His caress of your face turns with a false smile. He looks away for a moment and then comes back at you with a fist. You wake up with blood all over your face, drowning your eyes. You take the medicine like you're supposed to but sometimes you break, and you grab His neck and squeeze until he passes out at the wheel, and you smash the rail and drive off the highway. You survive because you unclipped his seatbelt and didn't have the roof of the car crush your skull."

Kika's eyes were unblinking. Her knuckles tight on the wheel, the car steady in her hands. Only then, did Mari take notice of the glyphs tattooed on her fingers and knuckles.

"See a cranky church lady," Kika said. "Now, there's a cunt who's never had a drink or been laid right. She holds signs to repent while giving you directions on how to get to Hell if you support abortionists. She's in that uncomfortable dress, old lady glasses, pointing fingers, face mean and pinched, waiting on Judgment Day."

"Was that you?"

"As a matter of fact, it was. Don't look at me like I'm disturbed. Think of me as having been given a strength to return from Hell to topple my enemies."

"Your enemies?"

"You don't see them? I'm not afraid to die. I either show love and affection, or I crush your face. There is no middle ground. I dream of being a fetus, begging my mother to abort me."

"Can you slow down?" Mari asked. "Stay in the lane."

"We're on our way out," Kika teased. "I'm not finished with Carbon yet, don't worry. You wanna get off now? Jump out any time."

"This is the way out of town, toward the landfill."

"We're on the high road to Hell, *perra*. There's an invisible fence around Carbon that won't let me leave until I finish what I came here to do. Don't you get it? You don't have to come with me. But you love Jubilee and now you're my accomplice. I already know the people we're dealing with. Go on, jump if you want. But I'm not slowing down."

# CH. TWENTY-ONE

Blitz checked his phone messages. A few texts from Phil and a message from someone named Slut#69. Soot drifted from the steaming remains of his blackened nightclub. He dusted his fancy, white sneakers while he waited.

"Fuck." He spat, walking corner-to-corner, trying to make sense of this shit, having no entourage for encouragement. Shading his eyes, he looked behind the police's safety tape. The club still smoldered in places. The wood bar was petrified charcoal. The plastic high tables and chairs melted and drooped onto checkered tiles.

"It's going to be months before that claim check comes," he mumbled to himself. "On God, I know this wasn't vandalism. I know what those motherfuckers are up to. When that payment drops, I'm gonna take my cut and run." He kicked the sidewalk and grunted. "All the pussy I tapped in here. All the drinking and snorting. All the shit I sold out the back…erased. Fuck."

He'd pimped his first girl from here after being promoted to door guy. A black girl, Juandira. Big-smiling girl, about six feet tall. She'd helped bring in more girls. His business expanded once his brother had him join the ranks, and then he just neglected the girls, especially Juandira, who soon vanished into the bell-end of a glass pipe.

Pacing corner-to-corner, occasionally stopping, and looking inside the blackened hole to make sure this was really the place, and that it had really burned. No other buildings around it had been torched.

The distant echo of his Sunday school teacher sounded in that empty space in the back of his head: "Jesus only loves those who are down. The weak shall inherit nothing…"

There was an impact, but he didn't feel it. At first. He felt his spirit leave his body, but, at that moment, felt no pain. His knees bent backwards in a most unnatural way. He was gutted by the hood of a car, arm caught in the grill. A vehicle traveling 65 miles an hour will do that. Cartwheeling in the air like a ragdoll, he thought, *Why would Honey drive her—my—car over the curb to run me over?*

Violent enough to evict his spirit, throwing his body in the air twenty feet above the pavement. A dream of carbon dioxide, a miasma of blood spray and spit.

Everything was clouds, moving in fast-motion.

Everything bright until blood flowed over his eyes and blinded him.

World turned black and star-speckled.

# CH. TWENTY-TWO

"Goddamn," Reynolds said as the car pulled into a pump station and convenient stop. He got out and stretched, dispersing ass wind. "I gotta take a massive shit. *Phew*. Jesus. Congratulations, it's a ten-pound baby boy…"

Chino drummed on the back of the seat. "Glad I can finally get out and stretch my legs."

"Nobody gets out of the car!" Reynolds leaned in, giving each of them a stare.

"Yo, boss, can I get an ICEE?" Garcia stuck his head out as he walked away.

"You want a piece of ice?" Reynolds momentarily stood between the gas pumps and shop entrance.

"No. Something cold and frozen."

"I'll get you a soda."

"It's not the same, boss."

"Well, you get one of those frozen drinks now and you're going to stain your ugly face. Then maybe you'll spill it on the seat of my car or, worse yet, on Miguelito's lap. You fuck up his Jordache straight-legs and it's your life. Then you'll probably be asking to use the bathroom when we're back on the highway."

"…Soda's fine."

"Hey, get me pork rinds," Miguelito shouted.

Reynolds stopped once more. "Am I the fucking gofer now?" He walked back to the car and threw a ball of cash at them. "Just you two guys. Get whatever they want."

Miguelito and Garcia followed him inside. While Reynolds walked to the back of the store into the bathroom, they went toward the coolers.

"Damn, we don't got stores like this in Jersey," Garcia said with wide-eyed wonder.

"You got 'em in Jacksonville, don't you?" Miguelito asked. He searched the rack of energy drinks and soda.

"Not like this, son," Garcia said. "Lookit this shit. A nacho fountain? Hot dogs. Taquitos. Holy shit. Breakfast taquitos? Damn, bro. Is this covered in the expense account?"

Miguelito looked at him. "Don't get greedy."

He walked to the next aisle. A minute later, he had an armful of junk food.

"*Sir.*"

Garcia looked around. A small Indian girl loaded donuts into a glass case. She was giving him a serious look.

"Sir," she said. "You're supposed to wear shoes when you enter the store."

Garcia chuckled, envisioning himself raising a family with this young girl and said, "I'm VIP, baby."

She didn't respond.

"All right," Garcia said. "Respect." He dropped his handful of snacks on Miguelito's arms and exited, whistling to himself. A big, black SUV swerved into the service station, barely missing him as he chuckled his way back to the car.

Abner gassed up. The Thunderbird was the only car at the four-pump island.

Garcia observed how compact he was as he went about his tasks and group chores. He washed the windshield and checked the tires. Made sure the car was shiny. "That store is badass, bro. You should see it," Garcia told Chino, who'd put his hands behind his head and closed his eyes. "That's it. I'm moving up here."

"All they got is farm work up here, bro." Chino kept his eyes closed.

"Nah, I'll be working for these dudes. I'm sure they can use all the help. Once they see what we do, we in for keeps, my man."

"I can guarantee you won't do anything," Chino said. "We're just going in to show his crew got bounce and we're nobody to fuck with. Maybe bust some jaws, but that's it."

Abner leaned into the car. "You two just sit back and let us do all the work. When we need you, we'll holler."

"What?" Chino laughed. "You gonna tag up against their midget brigade? You and that skinny motherfucker with the mustache supposed to handle all that shit by yourselves?"

"Maaaan, shut your fucking face." Abner waved him off. "We got other hard-hitters back home. You just don't know about them yet."

"All right. We shall see," said Chino. "I'll just stay back here, arms crossed, watching you get your ass beat, crying for your mama."

"Don't talk about my mama, *maricon*. She's dead."

"Yeah, when I put my dick in her, she exploded."

"Keep talking, pretty boy," Abner said. "Imma beat yo' ass and then teabag that pretty mouth of yours."

"You talk just like a faggot," said Chino. "When you're bent over, getting fucked by some Jamaican, Imma step in so you can suck my dick while they fill you up."

# CH. TWENTY-THREE

Strange synchronicity. The mouth of the universe was a giant gravity-well, spinning, attracting and luring all bodies into its centrifuge. Celestial, planetary, physical bodies. Everything and everyone magnetized, drawn close by coincidence, gravity, or colliding forces. The profundity of that went over Miguelito's head. There were moments where he didn't even understand coincidences.

And there she was, getting out of that old Toyota hatchback he'd bought her a month ago, wearing that maroon dress she'd worn to Reynolds' BBQ, and to the Christmas party he and his wife hosted last year. Not something to wear in the middle of the day in South Georgia, but she never looked sloppy. She smelled of lavender.

"Baby girl, why you here?" Miguelito asked, taken totally by surprise when Neesy saw him come out of the gas station. He was on high alert, eyes everywhere, carrying a paper bag of refreshments. Beneath one arm was a pack of chocolate snack-cakes and, under the other, a grape-flavored Colt 45.

He knew what the fabric of her dress would feel like against his skin. Against his face. Made him think of the Christmas party. Miguelito remembered that was the night she'd broken it off yet again with that creep Dale. He'd abandoned her right in front of Reynolds' place after the party and Miguelito had swept in, to the rescue. He'd taken her home and parked out front of her cinderblock house. In the car that he'd eventually gift to her, the same one now parked in front of the gas station. Through the curtains, he'd seen the silhouette of her elderly mother on the sofa in the living room. They'd steamed up the car and he'd groped her until they destroyed the backseat with their fornication.

"Baby girl, why you here?" Miguelito repeated.

"I don't know." Her giant hands wiped tears, smudging purple eyeshadow.

"Whatchoo mean, you don't know? Somebody kidnap you, drag you out here? How's your mother? The only reason to stop here is if you're on your way out of Carbon."

"So?"

"So, you had a fight with him again? Y'all always breaking up, huh?"

"He came to my job and started arguing with me. He got me fired. I packed my shit and left Carbon."

"Where you gonna go? Listen, stay with me." He went in to kiss but she dodged it. "Come on, baby. Let's go over here and talk."

They moved to the side of the building by the dumpster and an overgrown bougainvillea. He put the bag of snacks at his feet. He leaned in, licking his lips and reaching for her breasts.

"No." She pulled away but gave in a little, backed up against the wall.

He pushed and scooped in for a kiss. "I'm on the job now. I'm rolling with a crew. Otherwise, I'd drive you back to Carbon."

"But I don't wanna go back to Carbon," she said.

"That's where you grew up, baby. I'm about to make my riches there. What we got going on now, oh my Lord, you wouldn't believe what this trade is about to do for me, for us. I'll be free this weekend. Why don't you stay at my place?"

"I hate your dog," she said.

"Fuck the dog. I'll kick him outside."

"We tried this before. Remember?"

"Yeah, but you were still with Dale."

She turned off almost immediately. He may as well have told her bad news. "You'll do it to me again." She wept.

He backed away and just stared at her. "Things are getting more serious right now with this job, Neesy. Did you hear Phil got killed? Phil Davis, my boss? Don't tell nobody but, with Phil gone, I'm moving up. This'll be great for us both. Little by little, I'm getting up in there. First, it's Reynolds, then Blitz, then me. Me at the tippy-top. Can you believe that shit?"

"Who you here with?" She wiped her eyes again.

"Reynolds and a crew we just picked up. Bunch of guys from Florida."

"You went to Florida?"

"Yeah. Not to vacation or nothing. Strictly business."

The bougainvillea to her right moved and she froze.

A very tall, predatory black man with dreadlocks stood there, urinating. The fuchsia-colored bush was not enough to cover his size.

They made eyes and she was too startled to move.

He looked her up and down as he shook himself dry.

# CH. TWENTY-FOUR

"Look, look, look!"

Garcia's eyes lit up behind his thick glasses. Abner was in the car, engaged in small talk with them. Boxing. Beer. Pussy.

Chino's gaze went toward the station. Miguelito had pulled a fat woman to the side of the building and vanished. Two men got out of the SUV that, minutes ago, had almost run over Garcia. Two tall black men with long dreadlocks wore trench coats.

"Oh shit," Garcia said.

The taller one, skinnier and meaner-looking, with dreads to his waist, stretched his arms and legs as his partner entered the shop.

"Dude." Garcia looked on. "He's gotta be the shaman of the tribe. Look at that fucker. He's glowing like he's a magical wizard or something. I know you both must be thinking what I'm thinking."

Their collective eyes went straight across the lot.

"I don't know what the fuck's in your head," Abner said. "But that's mad suspicious. They're traveling the same road as us. Those gotta be enforcers on their way to Carbon. But who burned the club and killed our guys?"

"They infiltrated Carbon already, my man," Garcia said. "They setting traps while we sit here like chumps. We gotta intercept." He looked at Chino. "Right here, right now."

"I ain't moving until the boss commands it." Chino reclined, fingers knotted behind his head.

"If those niggers run into the boss in there," Garcia hyperbolized, "they'll kill him!"

"Nah, man." Abner couldn't take his eyes off them. "You gotta be a hard-hitting mufucka if you tryna slay Mr. Reynolds. But let's have a talk with them real quick. Introduce ourselves."

"I ain't going out there," Chino said, closing his eyes.

"When the shit goes down," Abner said, "I'll tell Mr. Reynolds you just sat back and did nothing."

"And what if that's not them?"

The taller one, the one Garcia referred to as a shaman, cased the parking lot. The man looked directly at them and made nothing of it.

"That fucker saw us!" Garcia pulled back and ducked behind the seat.

"When I say, 'Go,'" Abner said, "we drop the beans on him."

They watched as the other man casually walked into the shop. About thirty seconds later, he came out, complaining the toilet was occupied.

The taller man laughed and signaled him to go around the corner to the side of the building.

"Fuck," Garcia said. "He just told him to wait on the side there. Man, he's gonna spring on Reynolds when he comes out. He probably spotted him when he went inside. Holy shit."

# CH. TWENTY-FIVE

When the car stalled, Mari looked out across the smog-covered landfill, where it looked like war had demolished a city. It looked like the end of the world, and this was no dream. For a moment, she saw Honey's face again. She saw Blitz flying through the air and heard the crunch of his body when the car struck him.

Kika sat feverish beside her, sweating, whispering in tongues.

"What's left to do?" Mari asked, sick to her stomach.

Kika extended her arm and trapped her against the seat. She leaned and kissed her. She spoke into Mari's opened mouth. "I lay by myself sometimes, legs open, waiting for rats to crawl into me and eat me from the inside out."

# PERRAS MALAS

# CH. ONE

"Dat woman gon' drain you, f'you keep coming 'round to ha' like that," Bosco said, red-eyed and vaporous from the passenger side. The long highway gleamed ahead.

"Dat woman da mother of me son," Aries said. "What you expect me, just to take her out with a bang?"

Bosco had a big, white grin that took over his face. "Into a pasture and to the back of the head."

"Man. Listen to you."

"You can't, 'cause the music so damn loud."

Aries stroked the long, beaded braid under his chin and leaned in to shut off the radio. Hands back on the wheel, 10 and 2. "Nah, man. She don't deserve dat. She articulate."

"Like calling da state when the charbo late?" Bosco asked.

"Well, that says something 'bout me, don' it?" asked Aries. "She make sure da charbo on time."

"Man, fuck dat. You teach me it better not to plant a seed for fear dat the mother of child will eat me alive. I told you that black American woman very manipulative. You slight her but one time and it's ya funeral."

"You won't even date an island girl, meh son. You dating that Irish lass."

"She can't get enough of me, but she too Catholic to be Rasta."

"To be what?" Aries asked.

"To our lifestyle."

"You ain't no Rasta." Aries laughed. "Like hell. You been in da Bob too long."

"Yah, man," Bosco said in the most clichéd patois. They laughed.

Countless miles behind, many more ahead. Miami was worlds behind them.

When their laughter died, Bosco said, "So, you know how to use dem guns when we get dem? Dem ain't no pistols."

"Ain't much to dem," Aries said. He focused on the road.

"Lady don't like keeping dem 'round."

"Guns kill people," said Aries.

"Meh son, we kill people." Bosco laughed.

"Her mantra, not mine."

"Deez just as good." Bosco carried two axes inside his coat. And a short, black machete. Aries wore his machete strapped to his leg, which perfectly blended into his black clothes.

"Not for what Lady wants," said Aries.

"We bazadee, putting all this together for her."

"'F she weren't standing out in dat frontline with us, I would not bother. What are you in it for, Bosco?"

"Into what?"

"Into dis rample," Aries said.

"Just like everybody," Bosco said. "She done for me. And I do for her. She rescued me. Helped me family. No question 'bout it. But Lady want an army."

"She not 'bout territory. She know her place."

"We could lick down Ippolito without guns. You and I go, *Chop, chop, chop.*"

"Meh son, it's bigger than that," Aries said. "If you go up against him—chop and block—sure, but don't lie to yo'self. We need artillery too. Sometimes you can't beat dem with dem hand. Lady, she want all dem down."

"Rastas is all love and peace-lovin' kind." Bosco laughed. "We hug dem and pray."

Aries gave him a cut eye. "I'm a warrior for Jah, meh son. By all means, this shall be. I don't want no ting from these buckra we're meeting. But we need dem guns. Buckra got guns so we make dem deal."

"Streets made da man."

"I and I never ever lie. You know this. I was born, you can say it, privileged. I didn't approach da streets 'til later. My father was a police. He knew people. He knew people wanting to unbalance the status. Secret agents."

"CIA, you mean?"

"I can't disclose dat."

Bosco gave him a comical glance before they burst with laughter. "So, you can kill a man with just your hands if it come to it?" Bosco asked.

"Nah, I just look at them, all mean-like." Aries returned the glance and they laughed again.

# CH. TWO

Inside an old church established in the 7th Ward by Dominicans, all yellowed, cracked stucco and crumbling shingles, Lady Hennessey crossed herself, kissed her thumb and stood up. Illuminated by the temple's tall candles, she casted a long shadow up the aisle as she walked toward the exit. Kaleidoscope colors beamed from the stained-glass windows, as did the bleeding eyes of the crucified messiah from the cross above the altar.

She glimpsed at the creased photo in her hand once more before tucking it into the side pocket of her leather vest. Pictured were three young men with faces identical to hers. Similar cat eyes, charcoal complexion, and a love for gold jewelry and machetes. They were her spitting image. As if she'd manifested them alone, without their father's genetic input.

When she reached the pickup truck, Shank sat behind the wheel, singing and swinging her large gun back and forth like it was a microphone. A shiny beast of a gun, Glock 9, chrome-plated.

Lady stood near the window of the truck, looking in, watching, and waiting for her attention. When Shank didn't react, Lady pounded the glass. Shank waved her gun and danced all crazy gangsta, voodoo chile to the thumping dub beats. Startled by Lady, she froze and quickly tucked her prized piece at the front of her pants and pulled her shirt over it. Hers was quasi-paramilitary wear, like the men in her posse: black tank top, tribal branding, black tattoos, Saint Thomas flag for a belt buckle, and thin dreads hanging from under her maroon knitted cap. Accessorized with various knives and machetes.

She shut off the music and leaned over to open the door.

Lady seated herself and looked straight ahead. "You know why I asked you not to bring that?" Lady didn't have to look at her when she spoke, and Shank knew what was coming. Her brother, Bosco Lee, had warned her about Lady.

"But we gettin' a whole crateful a dem," Shank innocently pleaded in a way that made Lady want to backhand the young driver. "Mama, it's not loaded."

"Why carry it then?" Lady asked. "And brandish it? You gon' shoot somebody right now? C'mon, girl. Use common sense."

Unlike Shank, Lady's accent was Nola Creole sifted through an Alabama twang.

"Sorry, mama."

"Call me Lady. I told you already. Did you study the map? I don't wanna do no backtracking."

"It's all good. Phone show me where 'tis."

Lady drew a long, black cigarette from her shirt pocket and lit it. Smoke ruffled around her face. "It won't be too hard to find. It's a real shit-hole, where we're going. Pay attention to the road."

"Is all good." Shank smiled.

Lady pointed to an imaginary map in the air. She followed the highway all the way to the edge of Georgia until it fell close to the Atlantic.

Shank gave her a sarcastic thumbs-up.

"You talk to your brother?" Lady's rasp was leathery. She looked like a panther peering behind sedges of smoke.

"Nah," Shank said. "Talked to Aries while you was praying."

"Where they now?" Lady asked.

"They still in Florida. Caught some rain out of Odyssey."

"They gonna look crazy in them black raincoats, like they finna shoot up a bank."

"Dem no raincoats," Shank said. Her one gold tooth gleamed when she smiled.

"Whateva. We trying to make this clean and fast as possible."

"Aries had to drop off his kid before drivin'."

"Still having baby-mama drama?" Lady chuckled.

"Yeah, he cool. Shoulda murked da bitch long 'go but, seeing the kind of work he does, it is best the boy stay low."

"She cray-cray?"

"Called police on 'im," Shank said. "He suffer a month in da slammer. S'why he's got dem scars on his face. She scratched 'im up."

"Aries should know better than that," Lady said. "A man of dignity, honor. Talk slower, girl. Your patois is killin' me."

"Sorry," Shank said. "Want I should *pro-noun-see-ate?*"

"Fuck all that."

"Want to drive?"

"You serious? I brought you along to do one thing." Lady laughed. "Nah, just fuckin' witchoo. You good. Keep going."

"I brought dis Glock to protect you."

Lady sucked her teeth. "Mind the road, child. Imma let you sweat the small stuff. You can load that thing when we get there."

"I sweat the big stuff too, Miss Lady. And you don' drive at all? Make sense, I guess. You da queen."

"Uh boy," said Lady. "Forgot this your first time out. Best to just follow along. Listen, child. We just trading money for tools. Nobody's showing nobody up. They want money more than anything. We ain't fighting with them."

"Once we get there, we on our own," Shank said. "Plus, Aries and Bosco showing up strong."

"Uh-huh. You'll know when we get to Carbon," said Lady. "Town's just one big pile o' trash."

"Can't be worse than 'Bama."

"Oh, much worse, girl. But we in and then we out. No overnight stay in their stank motels. We got bigger shit to attend to."

"Back down to Florida den?" Shank asked.

"Best that we do. We go now, and they won't see us coming. Remember: We on our own."

"We go tomorrow?"

"We'll see. I'm aiming to get out of Carbon quick as I can, but the work is just beginning."

"What, five or six o' dem? *Pop, pop,* is over. I can do that me self."

Lady's laugh broke down to a cough. She relit her thin cigarette.

"Er'body thinks it's like the movies," Lady said. "Er'body think they Clint Eastwood. I got a few volunteers lined up, but they don' stand a chance with what we holding right now. They go up against them, just their big, scared eyes and medallions, these men we after get one look and they piss they pants laughing. When we go in, we going in like a lawnmower. Ruin them faces and they children's faces. I wouldn't send my crew to do a job I wouldn't do myself, but I wouldn't go in there with just a machete and good looks. We're going in armed to the teeth."

"What about da man in Polk City?" Shank asked.

"He got a group of cowboys that do this work, but they want the whole farm to do it. We can't afford him."

"Outsource. It's the American way."

"Too big. Cheaper to do it ourselves."

"But blood has no price."

"This blood ain't got that much money, girl," Lady said. "We tapped out going all in on this investment."

"Ain't you the one who said, 'If it ain't hard work, it ain't worth doin?' How 'bout dem people with da guns? They can't do it fa pay?"

"Don't know them other than what Aries said. He know they boss. Met him at some concert somewhere. They amateurs but they got tools to sell."

"The economics call for it," Shank said. "I get it."

"You got it, girl."

"So, once we got dem guns, we go back and handle dem that killed…"

Lady looked at her and it was enough that Shank practically melted in her seat.

"We have to prepare for it, not go in blind," Lady said. "I expect no casualties. Everybody comes back alive."

"Except dem."

"And they families. We'll run up on them when they having they Sunday brunch and fuck 'em up."

"I'm ready," Shank said.

"They won't know what hit them."

"Lady, I want to be the first to pop one."

"You just a driver, child."

Shank didn't argue. "In time," she said.

"You keep your eyes on the road there, girl. First, we make it there and get what we paying for. Because no guns, no war."

"Just happy to be coming along, Lady."

"You still young but I gotta break you in." Lady's face gestured elegantly like a sleeping panther, bejeweled and braided.

"You a legend, Lady."

"Is that what you heard? Ha."

"You made it out from where you came. That's heroic enough."

"By the grace of the Lord, I am here. I got another chance. My boys did not. This is for them. It should've been me. Don't ever get into a place where you walk away with regret. When you in, you do it and leave with everything you came in with or die with nothing."

Long roads ahead, two-lane roads and highways.

"That church back there?" Lady said. "Remember to always take time to thank God. Every day you wake up alive and breathing, you on the right track. Praise God."

Shank lit a thin cigar, drove, and drove. Eastward.

"Think your boys are up there, looking down at us?" Shank asked.

"They waitin'. 'Til we do this, they ain't getting' through them gates."

# CH. THREE

Aries unwrapped and lit a cigar he'd brought from Miami. He turned the music up in the SUV. The tranquility lasted all of one minute, when a gun went off nearby. He turned to look when the cigar was punched out of his mouth. Some crazy, white fool stuck his face and fists through the window. And then his friend showed up. Aries elbowed Garcia's face, but another fist came at him. Aries pulled back his right arm and planted a knuckle-row of gold rings across his face. Four and Garcia stumbled backward on the pavement.

Moments before, at the side of the gas station, Miguelito had drawn the snub-nose revolver he kept tucked in this sock and shot the man who'd been pissing into the bougainvillea.

Bosco took it in the collarbone but had already drawn a machete with his right hand. The little man and the fat woman had surprised him, and he hadn't time to zip up. Normally, Bosco used both hands, but his left arm was inoperable. A single, downward swing with the machete chopped Miguelito's gun arm at the elbow.

Before Neesy realized what was happening, she got a proper hosing from Miguelito's gushing stump. She backed away, sprinting, and screaming bloody murder all the way to her car. Abner and Garcia were beating on Aries through the SUV's window when she ran past them.

Miguelito hollered for his mother, palming the hemorrhaging stump. In his hemophilic daze, he tumbled to his knees, blood spurting between his fingers, reaching for the gun clenched in his severed limb.

Bosco grunted and growled like a beast searching for a splinter just out of reach. Thin blood-ribbons streamed from his neck. He stood over Miguelito with the machete raised above his head and came down on his neck bone. Bosco looked down at his crying face as if saying, "We're even," while holding the machete deep into Miguelito's neck. Miguelito drooled and soiled himself, lying in an expanding blood puddle.

Bosco put his boot to Miguelito's shoulder and yanked the blade out. Miguelito landed on his back. Bosco chopped again, this time into the edge of his shoulder, severing the whole arm. He yanked the machete and swung it sideways at Miguelito's throat once, twice, until his head came off.

Reynolds walked out of the gas station, holding a few items, feeling a few pounds lighter. He'd heard the gunshot and all the screaming and saw the fat chick get in her car and take off.

He mouthed her name, *Neesy?*

From this perspective, it was hard to tell what was what, and who was whom. A lot of back-and-forth confusion that his tired brain tried to link to some sort of narrative. Abner and the barefoot karate freak were punching a black man inside his truck. He heard screams from the side of the gas station.

When he rounded the corner, a tall, dreadlocked man was chopping Miguelito into loose chunks. Reynolds looked down at the diced Puerto Rican whose older brother, Enrico, had been a cook at the club when it had a kitchen, back when there'd been a club. Enrico, whose wife had cut off his cock and tossed it into the landfill upon finding his out-of-town hotel receipts where she'd never spent a night. Miguelito's older brother had killed her upon his return from the ER with the same knife she'd emasculated his brother with. Now, he sat like a eunuch Buddha in a Tattnall County jail cell, rotting for the rest of his life. Reynolds promised Enrico he would look after Miguelito and goddammit if he hadn't failed at that.

Bosco looked like he was melting, reeling from so much blood loss. His vision was going, his neck spouting.

Reynolds cradled Miguelito's severed head and sobbed. He grabbed the gun from the severed arm and emptied it into the mad machete man.

He placed the gun back where he found it, inside Miguelito's severed hand, still smoking.

# CH. FOUR

Those weren't rings, they were brass knuckles. Garcia had two ∞s stamped across his big forehead. He went back for more.

Abner received a full fist across his little peanut head that laid him out in the parking spot beside the SUV.

Aries slammed the door open on Garcia. He yelled for Bosco. More gunshots rang.

Then a tall, white man ran at him from the side of the building. He looked like a linebacker for the New York Jets, circa 1979.

Garcia yelled, scrambling back to the car, barely missing Aries' machete. "Chino! Chino!"

Reynolds slammed into Aries full force, knocking him against the SUV. He kicked the machete underneath it and lifted Abner with one arm and ran.

They crammed into the Thunderbird and peeled off.

Aries got back on his feet and ran to the side of the station. He'd suffered a few minor scratches and cuts. A small crowd grew around him. Bosco laid bullet-riddled, eyes wide open.

Aries crossed himself and kissed the wooden cross dangling around his neck. He rummaged through Bosco's pockets, removing all identifying documents. His friend, his brother in war, *mehson*, deserved a proper burial and departure, but he had to leave him behind.

# CH. FIVE

Kika casually stepped out of the car, like a celebrity sauntering down a red carpet under a starburst of white bulbs, except with bloodlust in her eyes. Using the hook end of the crowbar, she dragged Blitz off the sidewalk and into the street.

When he woke, his jaw locked. Shattered, really.

Kika drove her knees into his shoulders, grinding him into the pavement. Her duct-taped knuckles dropped on his face but, after a while, he wasn't feeling anything. The fiberglass front-end of the car had split. His body laid fractured, limbs twisted and pulled in unnatural directions.

"He was there." Mari spat in his face. Tears bulged in her black, glossy eyes. "He wasn't the one who put me in the car, but he was there. He runs the local drug posse. I shot his brother."

"Phil?" Blitz called out, spitting out teeth. "You killed Phil? We were going to build a kingdom here…"

"I think your trip is canceled." Kika stood over him. "I'm going to ask you where my sister is and you're going to tell me. That's all that concerns me right now."

"I see a car coming," Mari said.

Blitz groaned like a child, shitting, bleeding. His was face misaligned. One shoulder was higher than the other, legs turned inward. Broken, dislocated bones pierced his pants.

"Ask him again." Kika stepped on his throat.

"Wait, you'll kill him," Mari said.

"He's dead anyway."

"That girl from the party," Mari said. "The one you took with Billy Zombie. Where did you take her? What did you do with her?"

The childlike grimace on his face was not affected by his sudden deformity.

A car honked as it drove past, slowing to see the action.

Kika gave them both fingers and her tongue.

They kept driving.

Kika pointed at the charred, gutted nightclub. "Nice burn. I did that."

Mari looked at the black, gaping hole. "Did you know this is their club?"

"No. I was trying to torch the town, so I started here."

Mari grabbed a shard of glass from the gutter and placed it at his throat.

"Put it at his balls," Kika said.

"Where's the girl?" Mari pounded his chest and face.

"What?" His eyes were slits. "Bitch, you burned my club?"

Mari answered with a punch so hard, it shattered his front teeth.

"The girl you took from Billy Zombie's party," Mari said. "When you left the party with her and Billy, where did you take her?"

"Man..." He chewed his tongue. "She was with Billy. We partied. That's all... Condo... New condo. If she got lost on the way home, it's not my fault!"

Kika's heel at his plexus elicited the scream of a wounded pig.

"Wait!" Mari blocked her. "He knows."

"Jubilee is already dead, girl. Get it through your head." Kika walked away. When she came back, she pushed Mari off him. "We'll just leave you here, naked and dickless to the world. It's not really humiliating unless others are watching. I wish there were more people here to see me do this to you. Tell us where you took her, and it won't be so bad. I mean, we—I mean, *I*—will end it fast for you."

"Please—" Blitz gargled blood. "Don't kill me."

"So far we haven't left anybody breathing," Kika mentioned. "Is that okay with you? We'll beat you and dismantle you as needed. If you die, it's your fault. How quickly you go will be up to you."

"Stop," Blitz said through a beard of blood. "I know where she is. I know where. The Humps. She's... That's where they all go. The landfill. You smell it. You know where it is."

Kika dragged him to the car. Blood spilled as she lifted him. He fell with a splash and crunch into the backseat.

"Looks like rain," Mari said as Kika reversed into the street and sped forward. The car wobbled but she pushed it. It pulled a little to the right. The front axle grinded and the steering wheel shook. Three or four cars passed around them, honking.

"Tornados, maybe," Kika said. "You smell that?"

The sky went from pink to yellow.

"Yeah," Mari said. Gideon's Bible had been knocked off the dashboard. Mari picked it up and placed it between them on the seat.

"I don't dream of murder," Kika said. "It just goes hand in hand with my existence, like eating and shitting. Survival skills. Every human has a sharpened instinct for building a house for shelter, digging a well for water. Birthing. Healing. Killing. Disposing of the dead. You just tap into it, honey. Don't fear it. Don't fear when the animal wants to rip itself out of the cage."

# CH. SIX

"You talk to the chimney sweeper?" Seth sounded like he was beaming in from the other side of the world. "Where the fuck are you? You sound like you're a thousand miles away."

"Me? It's *you*, faggot," Funzo said. "Are you using a tin can and string to call me? Hello? You there? I can hardly hear you."

"Bad reception," Seth said. "Phil was supposed to meet up with Barry today."

"This is very last minute. Why can't you?"

"The trade, that's why. I'm heading toward the landfill right now. You gotta take over some of these things, you know. I can't be everywhere at once now that Phil is dead."

"Don't talk to me that way, asshole," Funzo said. "Like I don't have a job to do, too?"

"First things first. I'll take care of the meeting with the Jamaicans. You gotta hold Barry, though. He's got a flight schedule to keep, but hold him. We can be done with him today. Don't let him take off until the deal is done."

"That's your deal. He and I ain't so friendly. I'm running a little behind right now on account of some cleaning up I had to do. The shit hit several fans all at once, and I shouldn't even be talking about any of this on this line."

"Feds would have come in a long time ago if they were sniffing anything out," Seth said. "We're way beneath their radar. They should be the least of your worries."

"I'm not even considering that." Funzo grunted. "I've invested plenty of time burning documents and, you know, sweeping shit under the rug for you fuckers."

Seth sighed. "We're a skeleton crew right now. Things may not play out the way they were planned."

"We?" Funzo said. "You got a dead mouse in your pocket? It's us. Us out here with all this shit. Watch yourself with those Jamaicans. You go in there and if they feel you have other intentions, they'll smell fear all over you. You're not built for this."

"Who the fuck else is gonna do it, Detective? Who the fuck else?"

"Well, you've burned a lot of folks in your time. Don't ask who, but be prepared for what."

"We'll just wing it," Seth said.

"Reynolds will be here soon. He's gonna have the extra muscle. Don't sweat it."

"I'm not."

Funzo chuckled. "That's funny 'cause it sounds like your panties are in a knot."

"He's not here yet but I can't keep the Jamaicans waiting too long."

"You got Blanco?"

"Yeah. That fucking guy. I don't know about him..."

"All you need is his bulk, not his brain," Funzo said. "Phil wanted to flex. That was his plan all along. He wanted to show these outside families that he ran a legitimate business, and he shouldn't be fucked with. Now they've fucked around and drawn first blood. It could be ugly or it could go smoothly. Either way, stay vigilant. Look, you won't be alone. Stop talking shit, stop thinking shit. I'm telling you all this at no cost. But I ain't your fucking life coach."

"I never go into the field," Seth said. "It's not my job."

"Well," Funzo chuckled. "This is how it's going to run until shit gets back on track. Expose yourself a little more. You might actually get some respect from Reynolds and his crew. You sitting there, high and mighty, with your tie and shiny shoes in your office, looking down on us like we're wetbacks or something. I only stay in this shit-hole because I can't get out unless I burn all the bridges. Phil's dead now. In fact, his cold body is still on the morgue slab, he's so fresh. One of the reasons I'm locked down right now is because I gotta deal with that paperwork. I gotta stay clear for a while after all this."

The phone line whined and crackled.

"I need reassurance," Seth said.

"You want me to hold your hand?"

"You can hold my dick. Just get to Barry. That was the point of this conversation. Hold him. Get rid of the inventory and get the scratch. Pay off Barry and we're in. Hold him."

"I got no choice now, do I?" Funzo said. "I'll give him a hug for you, how's that?"

"If we lose this..." Seth said.

"We'll be free men."

"Free and broke. Still in debt to other investors."

"You get through this first part, and we'll do the rest," Funzo said. "Is that what you wanna hear?"

"I'm not asking for much," Seth said. "Let's be professionals here."

"Call me when it's done. I'll stall Barry so don't shit your pants."

Seth sounded tinny, in a vacuum. "On the way back, pick up Blitz. His car got torched. I left him in front of the club."

"Yeah, yeah. I got it," Funzo said.

"Hurry, okay?"

"Christ. Didn't you hear me? If I could, I'd be there now. Give me the signal you have the money, and I'll keep him there."

On the other side of town, driving toward the dump, Seth folded his phone and tucked it in his pocket.

Nestor Blanco sat beside him, cracking his knuckles and blowing raspberries. He looked like a shaved beast: giant forearms, jutting forehead, and crushed ears. Destined to be the middleweight champ until Abner put him down. But he could sing entire songs just by blowing his tongue trumpet. Loyal as a dog.

"When we get there," Seth told him, "we're going to take it easy and be civilized. Understand? Too many of our business family have died this week already. Loose and crazy isn't going to make us more friends."

Blanco nodded and cradled a fist in his left hand, occasionally glancing sideways at Seth. Occasionally blowing his tongue.

# CH. SEVEN

"Can't believe it. Can't fucking believe it!" Reynolds pounded the wheel with his palm, doing 100 on the highway.

His crew couldn't believe a man so large could cry, sobbing like a saddened grandmother.

"They killed Miguelito," he growled. "Just like that. What the fuck happened? Hey, asshole." He slapped Abner's head. "Wake up. You were third in charge after Miguelito. You were supposed to prevent this shit."

"Boss, those Jamaicans came out of nowhere!" Garcia was shiny and smelly with sweat. His mustache drooped over cracked lips.

"They had machetes." Chino kept looking back like they were being chased.

"Who?" Reynolds yelled. Windows down, wind and pollution blew inside the Thunderbird.

"The Jamaicans." Abner rubbed his neck.

"Fuck that. Where'd he go? Do you see him back there?"

"I told them to stay in the car, man," Chino said nonchalantly. The scar on his lip gave him a permanent smirk.

"Yeah and, when they were getting fucked up, you didn't even get out to stretch, much less help." Reynolds took a gun from his waistband and waved it around. "I should fucking shoot you right here, motherfucker. You let one of my best men go down."

"No! No, no!" Garcia waved his hands from the backseat. "Listen, listen. I told him to listen to you. I swear to God. I told him to obey on your orders."

"Yeah, boss." Chino raised his arms. "You said, 'Don't move.' You said, 'Don't move until I tell you!' So, I stayed put."

"I only saw two," Abner said. The brass knuckle stamp on his forehead was raised and irritated.

"Fuck all of you," Reynolds spat. "Miguelito got the other one. Miguelito was the hero today. He wasn't so lucky, but he'll be remembered. Jeez. Worst part is now I have to tell his brother in prison. Fuck. But I left his ass there. Had to. For shame. But we have to get back to town. It's on. Oh, yeah. It's on now."

Garcia smiled. "Hell yeah. It's on."

# CH. EIGHT

There were but two directions to drive into Carbon. Toward the landfill, or away from the landfill. Funzo was cruising past the airport in White Oak when he caught sight of two of his frequent contacts: Max and Gay J.

The two miscreants had been cruising the strip, which was usually deserted in the daytime, trying to make up their heads what to do with their day. Gay J was in rags. Max was Maxine today, wearing a dress over his jeans, his hair done up in sparkly braids, his face glittered and glossy with makeup. The day had just started for them, so, *Suck some random dick for quick cash? See who could collect the most cigarette butts that still had something left to smoke? Shoplift at the convenience store or—*

"Aye, up against the wall!" Funzo drove the car over the curb, pointing his gun out the passenger window.

"Whoa, whoa!" Max hid behind Gay J. "We're clean, man, we're clean!"

"No, you ain't, motherfucker," Funzo said. "You're scum. I can smell you all the way over here."

Gay J took a whiff of his armpits and agreed.

"Don't go with him, J," Max whispered.

"I don't want you stinking up my car," Funzo said. "Stay right where you are."

Gay J went up to the passenger window. "Your ride's a toilet, fat man."

"So's your face," Funzo said. "Listen to me: I'm going to drive up the block. Imma take a right where the mural is. I need a fix."

Gay J backed away. He and Maxine walked up the block, following Funzo's car down a narrow alleyway. The walls were covered in sloppy, indifferent graffiti. The bigger picture was an unfinished mural, abandoned years ago.

"Believe that shit?" Gay J pointed. "Didn't pay the artist so he just abandoned it. That's why we can't have nice things around here."

"Looks like shit," Maxine said.

"That's what I mean."

"I know. That's why I said it."

Funzo parked his car behind the building and met them face to face. They'd never seen him so sloppy and sweaty.

"Makes you think I'm holding?" Gay J said to Funzo.

"Either way, you're fucked," Funzo said. "If you're holding to use, I'll bust you. If you're holding to sell, I'll buy it, but I'm only paying one price and I'm taking the whole batch."

"*Maaaaan*, come on," Maxine said. "We're artists trying to make it here in the city. You're killing us."

"Well, I can kill you or have some of Reynolds' boys work you over," Funzo said. "Look, I don't have time for this shit. Gimme whatever you're holding."

"Well, we work for Reynolds too," Maxine said.

"*The fuck you do*," said Funzo. "You just pick up whatever scraps they throw at you and sell anyone out when there's cash in it for you. Whatchoo got?"

Gay J hesitated but dug into the front pocket of his hoodie. He withdrew an old sandwich bag filled with cookie crumbs.

Funzo snatched it. "This shit any good?"

"Same shit you bought last time," Maxine said. "Gets you higher if you stick it up your ass."

"Heh," Funzo said. "You wish, you fucking queer."

"Queer? That's supposed to hurt my feelings? Fuck yeah, I'm queer."

"Fuck outta my face." Funzo threw a crumbled $20 at them. He drove back in the alley, poking his head out. "Watch yourselves," he said. "Shit's going down. I don't want to see you fuckers on the strip for the rest of the day."

"You took our cookie crumbs," Gay J said. "Why would we keep cruising without merch?"

"Just stay the fuck off 'til the dust clears."

Funzo drove off and they each gave him the finger.

# CH. NINE

It'd been months since Funzo fashioned a smoking vessel out of aluminum foil and inhaled crystallized chemical smoke from it. If Carbon had a canned fragrance, it would smell of burnt crystal meth. And trash. And Carcass Bay. Every intake was a little bit of Carbon filling up his lungs. When it hit, his mind floated on a sea of steel wool until his fingers burned and he threw the foil out the window as he drove. He rinsed his mouth with yesterday's cold coffee. Anything to keep from vomiting.

He'd slept in the car. With his eyes opened. While driving. He swirled the coffee, drank and spit it out, convulsing with rage and repulsion. He pounded the wheel and dashboard, and even screamed at a wife who wasn't there. He floored it and Carbon got further behind him. Muddy cow fields to the west, the airport immediately to the east just as he missed the entrance. Cursing everybody's mother, he veered hard to the left, went over the grassy median, and curled back around, diagonally cutting into the airport, entering through the exit gate.

Three large hangars sat in the field, all of them painted gray. Half a dozen small planes on the tarmac. Funzo could see two figures prepping an older Cessna 172. One of them was fueling up while the other loaded the fastback rear cabin with suitcases, boxes of wine, and contraband.

Funzo put his brain on automatic, struggling through the crackling, blue meth static. He closed his eyes, rubbed them hard, took in deep breaths to the point of hyperventilation. He parked by the closest hangar and ran toward the plane. Pretty fast for being sloppy and out of shape. He knew how to use his weight to push himself where he needed to go.

Katrina stopped loading when she saw him coming and started laughing. She wore yellow coveralls and oxblood boots.

Barry was dressed for the beach, wearing shorts, a flashy floral shirt, and sunglasses. The sun had reddened the top of his shiny head. He shut the cabin door and wiped the windshield. "I was hoping to leave before you got here," Barry said. "I wanted to watch you run behind the plane when I took off."

"You going now? Couldn't wait one more day?" Funzo wiped his brow on his trench coat sleeve.

Barry looked out across the horizon. "Yeah. It's past my time here. I got other clients waiting, man. I can't just hang around here all day, waiting on you to come up with some scratch. This is my time and my dime."

"Where you off to?" Funzo asked.

"Back to Ft. Lauderdale," said Barry. "Where else?"

"Come on. We were good to you. Just one more day. In fact, just wait until the end of today. The deal is going down, as we speak. Look, I know we've had some deaths. Things are fucked up right now. The boys are restructuring."

"There's nothing further to discuss." Barry took inventory of what needed be loaded. "You're not looking so good there, Detective. Smells like you've been sleeping with pigs. This town is not where I want to do business anymore. I mean, I saw it coming. Jesus. You been at the dump again? 'Cause you smell like it."

"No. Not today."

Barry faced him. "Phil invites me here, sets me up all fancy, and then he's gone. What am I supposed to do? Look at it from my viewpoint, for fuck's sake. With Phil gone, I can't do business here. I hate this fucking place. I came out as a favor to a guy I did lines with in high school. And now he's dead. Takes a long time to build that trust again."

"These boys can start back up again with your exports," Funzo said. "Without product, there's no business."

"Don't worry, they got the girls and the dump business," Barry said. "In time, the club will be up and running. Really, there's only one reason to come to this town, but it's not the strip clubs. It's not the view either."

"Barry, who's gonna distribute up here for you?"

"You don't worry about that, Mr. Policeman. I got plenty of other channels I can go through. And don't cry about it. I'm sure you'll still be on their payroll, whether we strike up a partnership or not."

Funzo wiped sweat off his face with his palm. "I tell you, we got people. We can get this business done."

"Those hungry boxers you cart around? Are you kidding me?"

"Just one more afternoon. I swear," Funzo said. "It'll all be straightened out. I promise. We're just waiting on this other thing to go through. You're gonna regret turning this down."

"Look, you're a cop and all." Barry continued to load freight. "I… I don't know about this. I made up my mind a day after I got here. I knew it would fall apart, but I gave it a chance because I knew Phil."

"Come on, motherfucker. You love money. You can move right into town, open up your chimney cleaning business like we talked about."

"I don't clean chimneys," Barry said. "They're exhaust vents, as it happens. But I could be selling cookie jars on the side, for all it matters. I won't be doing it here. Listen, you really could use a bath. Two showers in fact. Burn those fucking clothes. Looking at you, it's hard to imagine you once had it all. Phil told me about you. Stripper wife. Decorated badge. What happened to you?" Barry shook a finger at him. "Every man builds a kingdom that will someday topple. There's no dodging all the fucked-up shit that comes with success. I know your son died. Wife disappeared. And I'm inclined to believe that she's out there somewhere, under a mountain of trash. You still collect from the Albanians, right? What does it matter, long as you're earning that buck, Detective?"

Katrina giggled and something in Funzo boiled over. He grabbed her arms and pushed her up against the plane.

She twisted from his grip, pulling a knife from her boot.

While he fumbled for his gun, she popped the blade in him just below his right nipple. A good four inches, through his encrusted trench coat, shirt, and ribcage. She stood three feet away from him, ready to do it again.

Funzo backed off, grunting. He drew his gun, but Barry drew his. Funzo pressed his left palm over the bleeding hole in his chest.

"Now, now." Barry began with his slow drawl. "I could pop you right here, you desperate bastard. But I will get a bigger thrill knowing you're stranded in this shit town forever. In fact, just the thought makes me smile. Those thoughts hit deeper than bullets."

"Fuck." Funzo went to shoot but didn't.

Barry shot at his feet. Katrina jumped out of the way, still pointing her bloody blade at the detective.

"Don't make me kill a cop, man." Barry stopped smiling. "If you shoot me, just consider that men in trench coats and fedoras will visit your town and clean you out. Consider it." He held his hands up like scales. "Cause. Affect. I'm not going to kill you, so I hope you didn't shit your pants. You don't need me anymore. You guys got it all under control. Remember that next time you wanna play with the big boys. Stick with what you know. This town is Hell, and this is where you'll spend eternity."

# CH. TEN

Ragged black dress, her hair a basket of angry snakes after the wind blew her hat away. Big, cheap sunglasses gave her an insect face. A whirlwind of crows circled, waiting to swaddle her in a cyclone of raging beaks and claws.

"It's just shit," Kika said. "Don't be scared. We're all shit."

The car was steaming. Not only out of gas, but the front axle had finally given up.

Blitz sat against the landfill's perimeter fence, behind which were mountains of trash.

Kika came at him, teeth and nails. She kicked him again and again. Pulverized him into the ground. After she'd gotten it out of him, gotten him to point in the general direction of where they stashed the bodies, she left him alone. Left him blind and disfigured, walking past the car, blood dripping from her hands and arms. She tossed his eyeballs to the crows. One of birds broke the circle and caught one in midair. The rest of them fought over the remaining eye where it landed on the road.

Mari held her hands over her head, fingers laced. Crows swept in closely.

"You know what I think?" Kika asked. She rested her chin on her bloody hand. Blood ran from her elbow to her feet. "I need to visit the local druggist and get new color for my hair. You too, girl. I'll go red, you go blonde. They won't know us, where we're going. Plus, you'll look and feel like a million bucks. At least that's what the commercials would have you believe."

They could barely hear each other over the deafening caws.

"Where are we going?" Mari was in tears.

Kika didn't answer. The mountains of garbage had once been small dunes and mounds. She remembered being a teenager and scouring the landscape for treasures. Old televisions, car parts, discarded cutlery. Being beaten with a coat hanger if nothing of value was found.

"If I could have one more day to see her," Mari said, "I'd probably be too sad because I'd have to say goodbye to her forever."

"Are you sad or just pitiful?" Kika asked.

"Neither. I'm beyond scared."

"You want to know where we're going? Follow me in here."

They walked through the gate, followed by crows and a few vultures.

"I knew some of these boys when I was a young girl growing up here," Kika said. Mari walked behind her. "I always thought a giant sinkhole would open up one day and swallow the whole town, consume all the sinners. I'd wondered about the people whose lives those boys would destroy. Possibly my own. When I kill them, I will destroy my past."

"Aren't you tired?" Mari asked. She was drained and pallid, bloody and dirty. "Haven't you done enough? Haven't you been redeemed?"

"I bled him for every miserable shit who deserves it but got away," Kika said. "Your hands are dirty too, girl."

Once they were through the gates, they followed the spiraling trail. Pyramids of scrap metal towered high above them from all sides. There was no sense to the structures, randomized across the field. Ahead stood monolithic cubes of crushed cars. In some places the ground broke, exposing a decades-old stratum of pressed garbage. The stench was a solid wall. They were oblivious to it.

Behind them, Blitz screamed one last time.

# CH. ELEVEN

Two ecstatic angels moved forward into the Mecca of trash, one holding a crowbar, the other a shredded bible. Carrion birds followed.

Mari walked beside her and gave her a long. hard look. The sun lit up Kika's visage, blood specked and sagging. She looked nothing like Jubilee. At times she was spectral, the shivering heat vapor of a desert ghost. Kika was a map of scars and bruises. She was the scar of vengeance, the scar of a wounded mind, the fetid and gangrenous lesion of a town's malevolent psyche.

Gunshots behind them.

Mari stopped. Blood sprayed her face.

Kika jerked forward and hit the ground. Blood spouted from her neck and shoulder. She gasped wordlessly, eyes locked with Mari's.

Mari stood very still, tightening her grip on the bible when the man in the long coat approached from behind.

"I'm a cop," Funzo yelled, pointing his gun. "Stay where you are, little girl. I will shoot you too." He had his thumb plugged into the hole below his nipple. Blood streamed down his coat and pants. His shirt had vanished in a screen of red.

Mari brought the bible closer to her chest. She hugged it, raising her crying eyes to the sun, beyond the thin clouds and into Heaven.

Only the crows and vultures looked down at her.

# CH. TWELVE

A thumb hooked in the wound was easier than trying to seal it. Inside, his car was slick with blood. Steering wheel, dashboard panel all sticky. He steered with his knees, dialing Blitz. The phone slipped from his hand, sliding beneath the seat. He drove right past the smoldering club and had to violently pull at the wheel to make the U-turn. The car climbed the sidewalk to the club corner. The spot that Blitz said he'd wait, but that motherfucker…

The wound in Funzo's chest felt like ground glass heartburn. That nipple would never look the same. He thought of Barry.

"Hope your fucking plane crashes over the Atlantic, motherfucker." Funzo cursed. "Stupid, black cunt." There was a surge of pain up his arm so sharp that he gritted his teeth. His right hand was numb. Shoulder paralyzed. Tears streamed down his dirty face. He leaned his head onto the wheel until it passed. Fell asleep for a few minutes.

Couldn't tell how long he'd been under. His neck was sweaty, hands shaking. He searched the street and sidewalk, nobody. Nothing. He reached in his pocket for more aluminum foil. Still had a few cookie crumbs left that he'd bought off those two creeps. The smoke was sweet and sugary. After two hits, he coughed until he puked between his legs.

He crawled out of the car, slammed the door. Skid marks stretched from the opposite direction, ending at his feet. The smell of burnt wood, corroded plastic, and brick coming from the club made him vomit again. He hadn't eaten since he couldn't remember when, so it was mostly coffee. While bent over, he inspected the skid marks then noticed his blood dripping where blood had dried to a paste on the street. He squatted and swiped a sample. He studied the tire marks. Small sports car. He looked in the gutter and found a white sneaker ruined by tire marks and blood streaks. There were teeth in the shoe and hair glued by blood to the curb. Jewelry. Thick gold chain and a pendant. A cross. Blitz's fucking jewelry. He grabbed them and shoved them in his left pocket.

"Fucking white nigger." Funzo took a deep phlegmatic breath, mouth open, and got to his feet.

In the car, he pulled out the chains and bounced them on his hand. Reminded him of his long-gone wife and her propensity for tacky bauble. He'd beaten her within the first few months she'd arrived from Croatia. He'd punched her and aimed his gun at her head. Starved her. She'd run off after that. At least, how he remembered it. The bodies were layered so deep in the strata of the landfill that it was easy to forget.

# CH. THIRTEEN

"I mean, he'll never know this joy," Maxine said to Gay J. "He can put his mouth to a tailpipe all day and get high off that, but he'll never know the simple joy of just hanging and dangling in front of a convenient store."

The pair loitered in the gas station parking lot, enjoying Diet Cokes and a chemically treated joint.

"Why do we need a beach or poolside?" Gay J asked. "We got what we need right here. They hate us, 'cause they wanna be us."

"Yup," Maxine said.

Later, they wandered off, strutting at their own pace, heading south. Smoking, vacillating.

"I don't know, man. That was pretty fucked up," Gay J said. "I might need something stronger after that to clear my head."

"True," said Maxine. "Plus, that burnt club is an eyesore." She puffed and passed, sipped Diet Coke.

"Bitch, you're an eyesore," Gay J said.

"Fuck you. You stood there and watched too."

"Fuck else was I gonna do?"

"I'm done with these vibes, man," Maxine said. "Keep walking. Need to clear my head."

"Let's walk the next block over. Don't want Bozo the Cop to give us shit."

"I hate that motherfucker."

"He's in with them," said Gay J. "He's super dirty."

They both made retching sounds.

"*Maaaan,* fuck this," Maxine said. "You believe this?"

"What?" Gay J asked.

Maxine nodded toward the street, at an oncoming car.

Funzo's unmarked trash bin cut across the avenue, going the wrong way. It jumped the sidewalk and forced them against the shuttered front of a knickknack shop. The stink emanating from his car was lethal.

Gay J and Maxine wrinkled their faces at Funzo, who pointed his gun at them.

"What I tell you freaks about walking the strip?" Funzo grunted.

"I mean," Gay J said, "where the fuck else we supposed to go, chief? We were just getting a drink. I mean, the man at the store appreciates our business. We were just stimulating the economy."

"The gas station?" Funzo said. "Across from the nightclub?"

"Across from the lump of charcoal that used to be the club?" Maxine said. They laughed.

"It's the only gas station in Carbon," said Gay J.

"What happened to Blitz?" asked Funzo. "I just drove past and he's not there. The lawyer should have dropped him off."

"Well, we kind of saw him," Gay J said. The two of them nervously glanced at each other.

"Was he getting high with you?" asked Funzo.

"Nah, man," Gay J said. "He never gets high with queers."

"Then where the fuck did he go?"

"He got a ride with two angry ladies. They kind of ran him over."

"What? What the fuck are you saying?"

Maxine said, "Looked like they were driving his old car."

"Which way did they go?"

Gay J and Maxine pointed in the direction of the landfill.

Funzo growled like a rabid dog and shot at them. He aimed for their feet but wounded Maxine's knee.

He'd never heard a human shriek like that and never wanted to again. He pulled the car back on the street and sped off, leaving Gay J and Maxine crying over each other.

# CH. FOURTEEN

Speeding down the central strip, Funzo dialed Blitz and left several obscene voice messages including, *"This is why your crew died. You weren't paying attention! You better call back soon, motherfucker. We lost Barry! The deal is broken! Fuck it. I'm going to grab some of the crates myself and head out to The Humps!"*

He took a short jaunt over the highway. Twenty minutes later, he arrived at the desolate maze of new developments, stopping at the smoldering pit where Embra used to live.

All that remained of her house was part of the frame and a chimney. The garage, in particular, was leveled.

"I just about expected that," he said without getting out of the car. He drove back the way he'd come, heading toward the landfill. The police bulb spun, silently red and blue as he angrily waved his gun inside the car.

# CH. FIFTEEN

Aries was doing 90, tightly holding the wheel, checking the rearview. That mint blip half a mile behind him was Reynolds in pursuit. Carbon was still forty miles ahead, but he could see the mountains of trash in the distance.

He placed his phone between ear and shoulder after dialing Shank. Lady Hennessey answered. He could hear Shank's music playing in the background.

"How goes it?" Lady Hennessey asked in her breathy, masculine timbre.

"No good," Aries spoke with a Virgin Islands accent that often had him pegged as Jamaican. "They surprise us. We got jumped."

"Was it any of Ippolito's men? Where?"

"We was south of Jacksonville. Stopped to gas up. Driving there was bad salt. That town is no good. Bosco is dead."

Silence.

He heard Lady Hennessey tell Shank to turn off the music.

"Hold up, what?" Lady asked.

Aries breathed out forcefully. "Murked at the gas stop. Dem men tackle me, but they run off."

"You shoot any of them?"

"Wasn't going to bring more attention to me self, Lady. Time I find Bosco, he shot dead. He got one of theirs doh."

"Who was it?" Lady asked.

"Not sure. Dem ragamuffin. Too boogu to be Ippolito's men. They boss man was buckra."

"A trap," Lady said. "Somehow Ippolito has people up here. They on to us."

"Never trus' buckra," Aries said.

"You mean a white man?"

"White devil, yeh."

"Y'all was at the wrong place, at the wrong time, child."

"Lady, hold back," Aries said. "Get out now if you can. I'm still a way away."

"We're already here. The man with the tools is on his way."

"Hold off long as you can. Might be a trap, as you say. May not be able to escape if they corner you."

"There is no question about that now," Lady said. "We deep in they territory. This town is tainted. It stinks. I feel its sinister current in my bones. It's sick and I don't want to be here longer than I need to. But we need them tools."

"I be there soon. Stay safe." Aries cut the line. He threw his phone on the passenger seat, immediately feeling the vast emptiness left by Bosco's absence.

# CH. SIXTEEN

Minutes later, Lady Hennessey explained Bosco's fate to Shank. Bosco had been the same age as she and they'd grown up orphans in Nazareth. People frequently mistook them for twins until his growth spurt made him a giant.

Parked among the scrap metal pyramids, hidden away from the rest of the city, they waited.

Shank jumped out, slammed the car door and stood beside it, screaming holy Hell.

Sitting very still on the passenger side, Lady Hennessey smoked her blunt. She watched Shank stomp and holler, violently stabbing her gun in the air, shaking angry tears from her face. Beating the ground with her fists, she cursed the very earth that bore her, like some possessed girl-child in this apocalyptic playground.

# CH. SEVENTEEN

Bleeding out, Funzo picked Kika up and carried her to his car. Mari walked in front of him, his gun at her back. "Open the trunk," he said.

Mari lifted the lid and stepped back.

The smell.

"Kind of crowded right now," Funzo said.

Flattened cardboard boxes lined the bottom of the boot. In one corner, there was a short-bladed chainsaw, pickaxe, and shovel. In the other corner were several rolls of garbage bags. Taking up most of the trunk was a body under a wool blanket. Funzo dropped Kika on top of it and shut the lid. Kika's dress hem flapped out, blood-crusted and muddy. "It won't matter," he said and grabbed Mari by the throat. He stuck his gun in his right coat pocket and told her, "Hands out front!" then zip-tied her wrists.

The bible fell from her hands. He picked it up and winced at its touch. He shoved her into the passenger seat and got behind the wheel. He threw the holy book at her.

"I'll let it comfort you since you delivered yourself," he said. "How perfect was that? At least something went right today. You little cunts killed Phil. How could you be so stupid? I got it all figured out. Did you burn that dyke in her house, too? You working alongside the Jamaicans? I recognize you from some of the protests, but I don't know who the bitch in the trunk is. Fucking savages. No gun crates, Barry's gone and bailed out, several crew people dead. Reynolds isn't here yet, otherwise I'd serve you to him first. And I really can't arrest you and just take you back to town. I want you to understand that. I want you to know I've considered every avenue available. Jesus, this fucking hurts."

He drove the car in and around the garbage maze.

"I'll let you dig your own hole," he said. "How's that as a parting gift?"

Mari stared blankly at the wasteland. She held the bible tight in her bound hands. She was calm.

"This is where you brought Jubilee," she said. "And all the others?"

"I don't know who that is." Funzo steered with a pained look. "I ran out of fucks to give a long time ago. You should've known you'd wind up here too. I never thought, never imagined in all my years of living so dirty, that this would become a business. It started out with my old partner, Luna. He's retired in Florida now, but we were partners in Atlanta. I had to transfer out to stay clean, and he wound up retired, with a pension. But I was always the one, having to clean it all up. Should have been a garbage man, all the fucking blood and shit I've washed off. Florida. That's where I should be right now. Maybe I should pay Luna a thank-you visit. Knock that mail-order bride off his lap and piss in his margarita."

Tires slowly rolled over the crunchy landscape.

"You're from around here," he said. "You know this is where everything winds up. Everything you ever owned and threw away. This is also where the unlucky ones, the ones God forgot, get disposed of. Dead hookers for government officials. Junkies we didn't want overcrowding the morgue. Bus-loads of immigrants that died coming here, looking for work. Drug dealers we cleaned out when Phil took over. Armenians. Albanians. Russians. The piles of bodies keep growing and growing. It's so easy to just get rid of everything in a mass grave. The city was already taking bribes to bring in out-of-state trash trucks, so why not add more to it? Who would know? This city is so desolate, nobody cares. I mean, *nobody* cares. It just looks like trash hills off the highway."

Mari felt herself sticking to the seat. Her sweat, his blood. Flies covered the seats and dashboard. They crowded around her ear and circled her mouth.

The car wobbled over dunes of trash. At one point, it stopped in a muddy patch and skidded, but he cursed the car out of it.

"Almost made you get out and push," he said.

Scrap pyramids reached several meters in height. Vans, cars, and trucks mashed and cubed. The rusted Grim Reaper of an earth-scooper towered over them.

"The graves are all marked strategically," Funzo said. He fingered the knife wound. Mari turned her head toward the rear of the car, hoping that Kika would somehow rise from the trunk and rescue her.

"I've been looking for her sister," Mari whispered. "I guess I'm going to meet her after all."

# CH. EIGHTEEN

Shank steamed at the wheel. Her tears fell, splashing her breasts, jewelry, and lap.

Lady held her gun for her but had placed a MAC 11 on the seat between them. "We on our own for now," Lady said. "We gonna do what we hafta, child. Shoot the first man you see coming, but do it nicely."

Shank lifted her tearful face. "How I'm s'pouse ta kill a man nicely?"

"Smile before you pull the trigger. Got me? *Praise God.*"

# CH. NINETEEN

The truck Aries drove wasn't built for speed, heavy as it was with supplies and a motorcycle he strapped under the bed cap. His eyes were on the left rearview more than the road. Swerving, dodging, cutting it close, barely missing other cars. This wasn't a reckless chase, more of an expedited pursuit. The Thunderbird was big and rectangular, but it hauled ass, aerodynamic or not. And it was gaining. Signal, lane change, signal, swerve. *Honk!* Clown car parade.

Aries slowed to 55. Out of the corner of his eye, he spotted a state trooper parked behind the Corvette it pulled over. The trooper stood on the shoulder, citing the driver. Aries' eyes shifted from the shoulder to the speedometer to the gas gauge. Floating on fumes. Bosco hadn't had a chance to fuel up.

Aries passed the trooper as a brontosaurus reared its head near an exit. The long plaster-neck looked weathered and sinister, poking out of the trees.

The truck was just at the edge of Carbon. Garbage humps grew larger in hazy proximity. Aries could smell them even with the windows closed. He took the exit, driving past a riverboat stranded in a giant mud lot. Mossy, empty, and rotting. Had once been a seafood restaurant. Covered in giant vines, moss, and kudzu. Behind it was an abandoned amusement park, Tyrannosaur World. The woodlands were overgrown, with the occasional trailer poking out of obscurity.

Down below *E*, Aries made an immediate right toward the park, then made a left down a narrow service road for two miles. He came to a stop at a high, wooden gate. The place had been vacant long enough that there was a thick layer of leaves and tree branches covering the parking lot and entrance roundabout. He parked under the shadow of a T-Rex, as the engine died. He placed his head on the wheel and prayed.

Several minutes later, he heard another car coming off the road. Big, mint-green car right out of a 1970s police show. You couldn't miss it. Aries saw them before they saw him. He scaled the gate, straddling the coil of barbed wire at the top. He made sure they saw him.

There was a lot of yelling inside the Thunderbird and, finally, Chino stepped out and walked toward the gate. Aries waited on the other side. He watched him approach but didn't run. He cracked his knuckles and stretched.

The Thunderbird pulled away, driving backward the way it came. Chino waved it off like a bug. His eyes followed as it drove up the service road toward the highway. He climbed the wooden gate, straddled the barbwire coil, and descended into Tyrannosaur World. Under the looming shadows of plaster and wire dinosaurs, the two fighters circled an overgrown fountain where the bricks were cracked.

"Look like you seent one too many Bruce Lee movies," Aries said, removing his coat and machetes.

Chino chuckled and got into a stance, the way he'd trained all those years. The way he'd practiced in front of his dojo mirror, at the mall demonstrations, in parking lot brawls, and from watching *Kung Fu Theater*. He leaned into his pose, ready to spring.

"Ha," said Aries. "Me too." He tightened his leather wristbands and, when Chino attacked with flying kicks and fists, Aries killed him with his bare hands. Was barely a fight. Aries blocked everything Chino threw at him, managed a lethal headlock that snapped his neck. He left him facedown by the fountain among the dinosaurs.

# CH. TWENTY

"That's not how you get to Carbon." Reynolds pressed hard against the steering wheel as if he wanted to smash through the front of the car. He was dialing multiple numbers in one hand, but nobody was answering. He saw the SUV take the exit where the plaster dinosaurs lived.

"He's diverting," a punch-dazed Abner said. "Easy for us. We got him."

Reynolds flew across three lanes to the exit. He flipped off a honking car. "When we get there, I want you karate freaks to spread out from both ends. Corner that motherfucker. We'll see how well your skills come in."

Chino looked at Garcia. "You stay, boss. I got this." Then to Reynolds, he said, "Yo, chief, let me out. I drew my own straw. I'll catch this lightweight for you. I could use the practice."

Reynolds looked at him in the rearview.

"Seth is by himself with Blanco," Reynolds said. "We need to be there now. We'll come back around for you when we're done. Otherwise, I'll send someone to get you. Got it?"

Chino saluted.

"We'll be short two men," Abner said. "Right back where we started. Goddamn. All this hustling and bustling for nothing."

"Shut up," Reynolds said. "We got this. You just sharpen your fucking pencil and stand by."

They arrived at the abandoned dinosaur park, driving slowly.

"Look at him!" Garcia practically jumped out the window. "That muthafucka's right there."

"Let me off," Chino said. "I got him."

"Let me go with you, bro."

Chino gave him a sharp look. "Garcia, bro. Stay with this crew. Show these motherfuckers how it's done, Jersey-style."

"All right," Garcia said. "All right. We should get matching tattoos when we're done here. Now, go kick his ass."

# CH. TWENTY-ONE

"That's them," Seth said. The sleek, black pickup faced them, parked 100 feet away.

Blanco looked at him, scratching his head.

"Go extend your hand to them," said Seth. "Welcome them to Carbon."

The boxer cracked his knuckles and blew a raspberry. "You the boss man," Blanco said, plugging a finger into his itchy ear. "You go out there first. Represent."

"But I drove here. Are you disobeying me?"

"I thought you was kidding," Blanco said. "I don't have to do anything you say. You just the lawyer. Mr. Phil is the real boss."

"Mr. Phil is in the morgue, idiot," Seth said. "What, are you scared to shake some hands? What are you scared of? We just have to stall them for a little while longer. Until the crates get here."

"So, yeah," Blanco said. "*We?* Let's you and me go. You plus me equals 'we.'"

"Reynolds will be here with the cavalry soon. Also, while Phil is dead, I'm the boss. Now, go out there and introduce yourself and then come back. Make sure it's all good."

"Technically, Reynolds is the second in command. Then Blitz." Blanco scratched his other ear. "Remember that party when Phil lined us all up to fight?"

"Which one?" Seth asked. "I haven't seen too many of them. Not really where I want to be all the time, with the air all moist with cologne and sweat."

"I fought that day," Blanco gloated. "And I heard you bet against me. Blitz told me. He said you bet it all against me."

"Well, I'd only just met you, man," Seth said. "The odds were stacked."

"I won that fight, boss. How much money did you lose that day?"

"Yeah, I lost. What's your point?"

"You're asking me to go out and possibly get shot at by some Jamaicans," Blanco said. "That's gonna hurt. Bullets hurt when they go into your body."

"I'm giving you a direct order, man," said Seth.

"You the boss here and now but you ain't my boss. You should go first. You're the smart one. You got the pretty, white face that they'll like."

"We got you for this job 'cause you're all muscle, bro. If I'm the face, then you're the fist, Mr. Blanco."

"Ha-ha," Blanco said. "Well, you go, and I'll be right behind you."

"You bring a gun?"

"Phil don't want us carrying no pieces. That's why he hired boxers. We work shit out with our knuckles. Said if we didn't know how to fight, may as well not come to work."

"Goddamn it." Seth went into the glove compartment and pulled out a .38 Special 4-inch, chrome-plated and fancy with a pearl handle. He opened the car door. The moment his left foot touched the soggy earth, he heard a quick *prrft*. A spray of bullets pocked his car's hood and windshield.

Having only shot rifles during hunting trips with his dad and uncles, he was not articulate with this sort of thing. Especially with a small revolver. Plus, he was just a lawyer. Two years fresh out of law school, cowering and blindly aiming at two women he'd never met. His hand shook with every shot as he rapidly emptied the cylinder.

One bullet fragmentized the pickup's windshield. Three went through the open passenger door and Lady Hennessey. Shank's Glock 9 was still in her hands when she hit the ground, blood spouting from her upper body and neck. Even her breast implants couldn't shield her.

Shank tumbled out of the driver's side. Her turn at Cowboys and Indians. She rolled up onto her feet and moved on Seth's car, holding the compact MAC 11. She wasn't smiling. The look of fear overtook Seth's confused face as he raised the spent pistol at her.

Dry *click*s.

Shank sprayed Seth where he stood until the clip was empty. Bullets zippered the car and she watched Seth timber into soft compost. Blanco popped open his door and took off running. He had blood on the left side of his face.

She dropped the clip and reloaded. "Come here, motherfucker!" She yelled as Blanco sprinted up the littered trail. The Uzi spurted.

He caught one on the shoulder and neck but kept running.

# CH. TWENTY-TWO

Even if it was ever found, the truck was registered under Bosco's alias. It belonged to a fraudulent man who was now dead.

Aries unlatched the tailgate and hatchback, extended the metal ramp. He rolled Bosco's Kawasaki down and mounted it. Nothing like the smaller scooters he'd ridden in St. Thomas. This was a rocket, and it almost took off without him when he revved it.

He caught it, tamed it, and aimed toward the road that took him to Carbon.

# CH. TWENTY-THREE

Sweat and steam form garbage vapors. The car continued around the landfill's serpentine trail, over loosely packed compost. At certain spots, the ground had the infirmity of a waterbed. The car drove past clusters of old shopping carts, rusted washing machines, and small mountains of discarded computer monitors.

Humidity steamed up the windshield.

Funzo put on a pair of greasy sunglasses, taken from one of Blitz's dead boys the other night.

"You don't seem too upset," he said. "Good. I've been surrounded by nothing but weeping pussies the last few days. I could use a break from that."

"This is Hell," Mari whispered. "I knew it from the beginning. Carbon is a black hole."

Funzo looked at her and chuckled. "When you ride into Carbon, it's on a one-way ticket. No going back."

A dip here, a raised dune there, and, finally, the car stopped at the precipice of a deep crater. Funzo yanked the emergency brake as the front bumper hovered over the edge of the pit. Motes, fissures, and piles of dirt surrounded them. Unfinished graves, with shovels poking out of them. Mass graves of varying sizes.

"Look at that hole. All nice and fresh," he said, looking over the steering wheel. "Our guys do good work, don't you think? They have one or two earth-movers, but most of these ditches were excavated using legitimate spic muscle. I told them to dig until they reached the depths of Hell, and it's been a Hell of a busy week. Go ahead and get out now. Take your holy book with you if you think it'll save your soul. Nice that you found God towards the end. Me? I don't believe in anything. And that keeps me sane."

His gun followed her to the edge of the deep, wide tomb. "Gettin' kind of crowded down there." Funzo poked her back with it.

The stench from below was a fist to the nose.

Looking down into the pit, she puzzled over several maimed and pulverized bodies. Hollowed eye sockets stared back. Some had faded, strangled faces, and dislocated limbs. She locked eyes with

Billy Zombie's decapitated head. Dear dead Nikki, a strangled Ophelia in her red wedding dress.

Their presence did not stir the crows digging into soft body parts.

"You brought her here," Mari said, face collapsed with sadness. Her bound hands clenched the bible for all its worthlessness.

"Was she the blonde in the wedding dress?" Funzo asked, looking down at the grave.

Mari sobbed. "No."

"We had a bucketful that night. Goddamn. I'm going to need your help with this load. Come on."

He popped the trunk, yanked the keys from the ignition, and stuffed them in his coat pocket. He kept the gun aimed at her, left thumb plugged back in his erogenous wound.

"Go on, open it," he ordered, standing a few feet from the car.

Standing beneath the lid, she pulled back the blanket and there they were, sisters lying side by side. Bloody and mishandled. Jubilee showed signs of trauma to her chest and neck. Clothes torn and frayed, but they'd been kind enough to spare her lovely, emaciated face.

Mari leaned in and touched it. Jubilee's throat moved. Her chest slowly raised. Mari quivered a smile.

"Save your prayers for the pit." Funzo pulled her back. "Pull this one out first. The one I shot."

Mari hesitated.

He reached around his belt, where he'd hooked Kika's tire iron. It was slick with blood. "You killed Blitz with this," Funzo said. "Goddamn your brutality. Goddamn you, you fucking filthy bitches." He threw it over his shoulder, where it fell into one of the smaller pits. "Yank her out until her feet hit the dirt and then drag her to the hole. I will probably shoot you before I put my gun down to help you, so don't ask. But I'll let you say one last goodbye to your friends and let you pray before I throw you in there."

Mari nodded and handed him the bible.

"Get that out of my face," he said. "I don't fucking need that! You want last rites or something? What the fuck's in there for me?"

She opened the faux-leather cover, fingering the first few pages. Her hand plunged into the abysmal book, curling around the trigger of the hidden gun. The bible exploded. Just like she'd done with Phil, she blindly pulled the trigger—this time, until the chamber was empty. Bullets struck Funzo's midsection and right arm. He sloppily folded to the ground, under a rain of canonical confetti.

From this angle, he managed a few shots at her. Bullets struck the trunk lid, bumper, and top of the fender, but missed Mari.

She squatted on the side of the car, hugged her knees, and closed her eyes. Another bullet flattened the rear tire beside her.

He laid on his side, groaning like roadkill. Breaths quick and hollow, like wind in a cave. She could swear the bullet holes whistled.

"I see you, cunt," he said.

From the other side of the car, Mari heard someone. She looked underneath and saw a blur of sneakers. A flustered, crying man ran by screaming, "*¡Perras malas!* She's coming! *Dios mio!*"

Blanco ran past her and tripped, swallowed by one of the open graves.

Funzo stood up. His right arm cascaded blood from two separate holes. He held in his guts, keeping his balance. "That dumb motherfucker will die today." Funzo wheezed. "You can just tell. Hey, come back! Blanco, it's me, the detective! Help me to bury these cunts!"

More footsteps.

Shank appeared behind the detective, wielding two machetes.

Funzo slowly turned and she chopped off his gun hand. With an audible *fauk*, hand and gun curved the air into one of the open pits. He hadn't the lung capacity to scream.

With the same momentum, Shank diagonally wedged a blade into his face.

His jawbone flapped open, and he vomited tongue and teeth. He grabbed at his face with his bloody stump, circling dizzily, spurting blood, eyes exploding from his head. He grabbed at her with his remaining hand, but she feinted.

Shank leaned into him, crossing both machetes at his neck, removing his head. Then she whacked one arm off, then the remains of the other. She whacked until he was reduced to a bloody stump.

After which, silence. She pulled back, breathing, sweating, dripping blood.

For a few seconds, everything was still, gentle. Even the crows were quiet. Perched but curious. Slowly, the fragile earth let out a low, pained moan. The drone of a wounded beast.

Blanco, groaning from the hole where he'd fallen.

He yelled, "Funzo, I think I broke my foot. *Ayyy!*"

Shank rounded the car, dripping blades raised at Mari.

The girl sat on the ground, holding a tattered bible. The top edge of the book had burned and blew away. A gun barrel poked from the ragged pages. "Can you help me bury them?" Mari asked.

Shank scanned the surrounding open graves. So many of them. "First we kill them. *All* of them. Then I will help you."

# CH. TWENTY-FOUR

Standing against the car, Mari watched Shank drop into the pit. Blanco howled like an old, wounded dog. Mari could see the tips of the machete raise out of the hole. One blade, two blades, *chop, chop*, and Blanco finally quieted.

Shank climbed back up and walked toward Mari, machetes crossed at her chest. She looked straight into her eyes. "Are you the whores of these men?" Shank wiped the blades against her thighs.

"No," Mari said. Her face was a palette of mud, sweat, and blood. "No. We're not."

"Are they dead?" Shank thumbed the trunk of the car.

Mari shrugged.

"There will be others coming." Shank cut her ties then helped her pull Jubilee and Kika out of the trunk. Jubilee was bruised purple and black. Mari felt her low pulse. Kika was rubricated in blood that turned dark mahogany. Her face, neck, dress, and arms were caked with it. When they lifted her out, she kicked a fit and spazzed. She spat blood and screamed, tearing herself from their grip. Shank and Mari let her fall, one superstitious of the dead rising, the other just out of her mind.

They stood, watching Kika slowly assemble herself. Shivering, finding her balance. She took a few steps, palming the wound at her neck, soundlessly moving her mouth. She poked a finger through the hole at her neck to confirm the bullet's exit. She gritted her teeth and spat, going in circles until the light came back on inside her head.

Jubilee laid battered and frail behind the car.

Kika kneeled beside her and whispered to her face, stroking her matted hair. She held a long silence until, in the distance, someone turned on a radio.

# CH. TWENTY-FIVE

Crows. More crows than they'd ever seen.

"That's Honey's car," Reynolds said, death grip on the steering wheel. "I'm guessing Embra's here. Good. She brought the guns and the deal's going down. We're going to wipe the floor with them, gentlemen."

Abner eyed Garcia skeptically.

"I ain't never seen a crow that big!" Garcia said.

"That's 'cause it's a vulture, stupid."

Reynolds parked behind the battered, white car. They got out immediately.

Pecking crows, greedy and courageous, competed with smothering flies.

Garcia let the boom box dangle from his hand. His face was serious but cautious as he followed Reynolds and Abner, barefoot.

"The fuck is that?" Abner shaded his eyes.

Reynolds pointed while walking ahead. He recognized the one white sneaker and started dry heaving. Uncontrollably, like an infant. Convulsing. He started coughing but couldn't vomit. He roared and shot at the carrion birds that scattered.

"Oh, my fucking God." Garcia covered his mouth. "Who is that? What is that?"

Reynolds looked at Abner and walked back to the Thunderbird.

"Damn. That's fucked up," Abner said.

"They got ahead of us." Reynolds dialed Seth but it went to voicemail. The same with Funzo. "Call Chino."

"Uh," Garcia said. "Chino don't carry no phone. That's why you go through me. He says phones interrupt his meditations."

They got back in the car. Reynolds cranked it and drove into the landfill.

"We should come back and bury your mans," Garcia said. "He doesn't deserve to be left for the crows and rats."

"You can bury him when we come out, homie," Abner said.

"Yo, this place stank." Garcia covered his mouth. Flies crawled over his arms and forehead. They tangled in his messy curls.

"*That's what I told your mother,*" Abner said.

"Hey, man. Fuck you. Talk about my father but not my mother."

The car rounded the trash dunes, fishtailing. All eyes on the lookout. Crows greeted them with deafening squawks. A loose dog and a group of rats scurried by. The AC gave out at some point, but the windows stayed rolled up. The smell of sour garbage permeated the car. It was on their skin and in their hair. They could taste it.

"Jesus," Reynolds said. "Seems every time I drive here, the landscape has rearranged itself. Funzo's the one with the map for all this."

Ghostly fumes floated from a mountain of old television sets. Hundreds of them, sky-high. Rats and seagulls fought for scraps. An ear. A finger. Scavengers ran off when Reynolds parked behind Seth's white car.

The windows were shot out, bullet holes riddled the inside and outside of it. Seth laid facedown, holding his .38, one foot still inside the car. They could see the shit stains in the back of his pants.

# CH. TWENTY-SIX

"Thrown out like so much trash," Kika said hoarsely.

Fading in. Feet firm on the squishy ground. Fists tightly balled. Crows overhead. Seagulls squawking. Rats approaching. Vultures waiting their turn at last.

# CH. TWENTY-SEVEN

They approached Seth's car.

"You trading guns with these people?" Garcia asked. "Is that what this is?"

No one answered. East side of the landfill, someone was screaming.

"That's Blanco," Reynolds said. He was pale and sweaty.

"How many you think, boss?" Abner asked as toxic fumes choked him. White spit gathered at the corners of his mouth and his eyes watered.

"Supposed to be between two and five. We already met two of them earlier today." Reynolds inspected the bullet-zippered car door. "Goddamn." He didn't bother touching Seth. "Fuck a mass grave. We'll burn them in a pile. Jesus."

"These people gonna be missed," said Garcia, toes deep in sludge.

Reynolds slowly walked to the black pickup. Next to it was a dead woman. Stone-faced, black hair thick as rope. In dying, her skin had gone gray, like an ancient idol of unknown origin. She faced the sky, eyes open, having a final petition with her maker. Her open mouth was a gleaming cave of gold.

"Yo." Abner stepped up behind Reynolds. "I'm taking her shit. I don't give a fuck she dead or not. Look at them chains, bro. Lookit her rings. I said, Goddamn! Yo, help me get this grill out her mouth!"

"Fuck outta here," Reynolds said. "I'm not doing that."

"That's mad niggerish, man," Garcia said while searching for loot in Seth's car.

"That's how we do shit 'round here, thug." Abner grabbed bloody gold chains off her neck, jewels from her arms and hands. Took her gold lighter, her long cigarettes, even her weed. Draped the chains around his neck. Slid the rings on his fingers. Stuffed his pockets with the rest. Took her gun as his own but left her teeth intact.

Reynolds pulled out his gun and nodded at Abner. "Take that trail. Garcia take the other and I'll go between the cars." He pointed toward the scream. "We'll meet up on the other side by the fence. Kill on sight. No mercy. Fuck them up, whoever they are. They'll get you if you don't get them. Let's move. Pretend this is Vietnam. *Search and destroy.*"

Slowly, they searched the garbage dunes. For snipers or machete-wielding pirates.

# CH. TWENTY-EIGHT

Blanco's scream made Abner remember one of the first times they worked together. Some cleanup work for Reynolds, on behalf of Phil. The job had gone slick as garbage juice, and it endeared Blanco to Abner since they were no longer allowed to clobber each other in the ring. They'd been thin and tapered back then, lean, mean, hungry dogs. Fresh off the boat, slick with sparring sweat, and willing to do anything for money.

Abner had driven a van into The Humps.

"I thought they said we'd be stocking meat in the club kitchen," Blanco said. His facial tic made it look like he was always smiling.

"What do you think we doing?" asked Abner.

Blanco surveyed their cargo. There were a dozen dead sex workers rolled tightly in large swashes of Cling Wrap, their shocked faces visible through the plastic.

"*Ese*, you should cut a hole in the plastic and do it to them," Blanco said, blowing a raspberry.

"Man, you can't fuck a dead girl," Abner said. "She'll shit all over you. Plus, your dick will probably break off inside her."

"Word?" Blanco said. "I'm just interested in the front. Where you put a baby. And how you know? You fucked dead pussy before?"

"Happened to somebody I know. And it don't matter. Front, back, it don't matter. Just saying, put it in the back and she'll definitely shit on you. Put it in front and she gonna clamp down and rip your *pinga* off."

"You tried it, *ese*?" Blanco's tongue dangled out his mouth.

"Don't call me *ese*, homeboy. I ain't fucked no dead hoe. Never have, never will. I just heard from somebody who did. I fuck girls who have a pulse. How you gonna fuck cold, dead pussy, man?"

They'd found the spot, spent an hour and a half digging a grave big enough to accommodate a dozen thawing corpses.

"Carbon gonna run out of street-girls," Blanco said.

"They not all from Carbon," said Abner. "These bitches come from all over. Even as far as Russia. That's what we do here. That's the business, 'cause the coke is shit, meth'll kill you, the restaurants all suck, and the strip joints smell like catfish. But we got this garbage dump here."

"You know when we're getting paid?"

"Nope," said Abner. "Boss is still building up his growth."

"What that means?"

"It means he ain't rich yet. He's gotta build it up, know what I mean? You lose money at the beginning of any investment. He's trying to attract income from wherever it comes."

"But we gettin' paid, right?" asked Blanco. "I mean, we work. We need our pay."

"Yeah, man," Abner said. "You'll get paid. Eventually. You at least get a free meal and lap dance at the club."

"Dang." Blanco scratched his head. "They been at this, what? Seven, eight months? All I seen is what I get after a fight. Now they opening up a club and can't none of us get paid yet? They buy cars, we get no raise. I ain't got a car. I had you come pick me up."

"It's about loyalty, man," Abner said. "You know we'd be working in some field somewhere, picking corn and strawberries with a bunch of beaners if it wasn't for them. And you shouldn't even drive, so don't complain about it, knucklehead."

"Oh yeah, ha-ha," said Blanco. "True. Doctor said I took too many hits in my head and that driving is dangerous." He smacked the side of his head and blew a raspberry.

"You lucky they didn't retire you altogether, bro." Abner put a finger gun to his head. "Think about that and thank Phil and Blitz and Reynolds every time you see them. Thank them for putting you somewhere that you're not picking a field, or on the street, old, busted, and forgotten."

"Well, yeah. I'll thank them," Blanco said. "But they still ain't pay me none. I got child support to pay. The two brothers acting like broke chumps. They got dump in they pants."

When all the dead girls were laid in the grave, they shoveled dirt nice and tight over them. Blanco stomped the ground a few times and gave Abner a thumbs-up. Late that evening, they'd driven off, heading back to town. Abner could drive this route blindfolded.

"I'm hungry, *ese*," Blanco said.

Abner forgave him on account of the beatings. Some from his own fists. "We can eat after we shower."

"Yo, I want Chinese."

"Nah, that's like ten miles out."

"How 'bout that country place with the redneck cooks?"

"The all-you-can-eat joint?"

"On Thursdays, it's all-you-can-eat. Chicken's good but the last time I got a stack I couldn't even finish it. And then they won't let you take leftovers home."

"You gonna get fat, bro." Abner laughed. "They put shit in the food to fill you up. MSG and shit. Me? I always get my money's worth. I always eat an ass-load when I go."

"So, we always gonna be doing this kinda work?"

"Depends. Other shit will come up. It's up to you and how much you want to contribute to the organization and what sacrifices you're willing to make."

# CH. TWENTY-NINE

Wasn't too far from where Abner walked now, about twenty feet from where they'd buried those prostitutes.

"Reynolds, I want to tell you something." Abner's voice echoed. They'd lost each other in the maze of stacked junkers.

Reynolds paced, aiming his gun everywhere all at once. He looked over both shoulders, carefully stepping between walls of flattened cars stacked thirty feet high. "What'd you say, champ?" He could see Abner's shirt through the wall of mangled cars.

"I wanna get back into the circuit," Abner said. "Don't want nobody shutting down my boxing career again. I'm a champ. You said that to me."

"You were our best featherweight," Reynolds said. Eyes searching everywhere. He pressed close to the skeleton of a school bus and a faded ice-cream truck with missing tires, doors, and hatch lids. The ice-cream cone logo had been graffitied into a long penis with testicles.

"I know." Abner sounded on the brink of tears. "You wore us out like dogs, but we loved it. I promise, we did."

"I know you did, champ. You moved pretty fucking fast, little as you are."

"You seeing anything on your side?" Abner asked.

"No. You?"

"Nothing. Think they can hear us? I feel like I'm being watched."

"Keep your voice down," said Reynolds. "Yell if you see something."

Nearby, a sound like *hut!* and then an agonized scream. And then *hut!* again. No more screaming.

"*Abner?*" Reynolds called. Ahead, squishy footfalls beyond the stack of crunched cars and loud music. He stopped at the open end of the maze.

Garcia approached, blasting his boom box. "You hear that?"

Reynolds shook his head. "Can't hear shit over your music."

"Oh." Garcia cut off the radio. "Thought someone said something," he whispered. "There's a car over there. Looks like a cop car but with no lights."

"Buick?" Reynolds asked.

"I think so."

Reynolds loosened up. Just so… "That's Detective Funzo," he said. "And I use the term 'detective' loosely."

They walked toward Funzo's car.

"Put that stupid radio down, you idiot." Reynolds said.

"It's one of my weapons, boss," Garcia said. "I carry it for safety."

"Safety? You wanna borrow my other gun?"

"I don't use them. Goes against my Bushido Code."

Reynolds pressed a finger against his lips. They paused. Something wasn't right about Funzo's car. Crows perched on the roof, silently staring. Two broke off and swept down at them as if to scoop out their brains. "You go first," Reynolds told Garcia. Flies drank of his sweat.

"*Santa Maria, Santa Maria*," Garcia chanted as he went toward the car. A beard of flies thickened on his face. Crawled on his brow, his arms. Buzzing like a power box. "That's it, man. They're everywhere, watching. I feel their eyes. When they come, Imma give 'em the whole package. Imma fuck 'em up!"

"Who?" Reynolds asked.

"I don't know," answered Garcia. "Whoever is here."

Fires burned in some of the pits. Temperature escalated with the smoke. Flies were angry and incessant.

"It's just a hole with lots of dead people," Garcia mumbled.

Reynolds was silent.

"Just dead bodies," Garcia said.

"Abner," Reynolds called. "Where the fuck are you?"

Garcia looked to him for instruction.

Reynolds signaled with a nod, and they walked around the mass grave. Crows flew at their faces and regrouped outside the hole.

"Yo, that's fucked up," Garcia said after one glance into the pit.

"Let's go back." Reynolds waved.

Another fire bloomed near them, and Garcia ran, disappearing back into the maze of junkers.

Reynolds held his breath and took off after him.

# CH. THIRTY

Convinced something or someone was chasing him, Garcia didn't look back. He was trailing a line of piss, slipping on wet compost, trampling glass and metal debris that cleated the bottom of his feet. He called out for Jesus, he called out for Santa Maria, he called out for his mother (also named Maria). He ran until he dead-ended into a mountain of tires. A rat had drowned in rainwater inside a truck tire at his feet. As he climbed up the mountain, he slipped and cut his foot open. He limped around, mumbling to himself, looking up and around for an exit.

"No biggie, no biggie. Is cool, is cool."

The unstable wall of cars made a strained, wrenching sound and he stood there with a wide, frightened grimace. He looked up, mouth agape, glasses slipping back against his face. The last thing he saw was an avalanche of crushed cars coming down on him.

# CH. THIRTY-ONE

Reynolds came running, shooting in the direction of the avalanche. Crows swarmed and pecked his face, flying out of crevices between junkers and scrap metal, diving out of the sky. He found himself cornered, blocked by tires and stacked cars, swarmed by pecking rooks. There was a slim gap between the cars just ahead. When the birds cleared and began circling him, he could see an exit down the narrow end.

"Hey, man," Reynolds said. He reloaded. "You there? *Karate Man*, where the fuck are you? *Abner?*"

Junkers shifted and scraped. Metal creaked and groaned. He smelled smoke. As the cawing died down, he heard a commotion on the other side of the stacked cars. Whispers and low voices. Boot steps over rusted steel and iron. The cry of strained metal.

"*Fuck you!*" Reynolds aimed and shot at the empty spaces. He stood, bleeding from cuts and scratches, feathers in his mouth.

The shadow passed over him like a death angel. For a second, he thought it was a vulture.

Balancing on a triple stack of junkers was Shank. Handkerchief covering half her face, dreadlocks twirling as she shook her head. Lady Hennessey's bloody gold chains dangled around her neck. Smoke plumed behind her as she teetered the top car. Rocking to and from, close to the edge, just above him. Machetes drawn.

Reynolds aimed at her and shot until his gun was empty. Instead of reloading, he threw it at her as hard as he could, but she had vanished in the haze. He rushed forward and squeezed sideways into the gap between cars. "*Abner,*" he yelled. He saw her shadow again and moved further in until he was stuck. Trapped by his big belly. He tried climbing the side of the car but his mud-caked Irvine Park loafers had no traction. To his left, the exit was several car spaces away. He'd underestimated the width of the crosscut. Violently jerking, he caught the wrath of the chromium door trim, tearing his thigh open, howl echoing across the scrapyard.

He tried going back to the pile of tires, but his legs squeezed in too tightly. He grabbed the top of the car for purchase but the rusted edge cut his hands. He grunted and closed his eyes, blood trickling down his elbows. When he opened them, he looked inside the car. There was a dead passenger in the seat and it was Abner.

Eyes open, face was at peace, but his neck tilted unnaturally sideways. The side of his head had been crushed with a car battery. The jewelry he'd snatched from the dead woman, removed.

Reynolds shook his head in disbelief. Smoke choked him up. He stared at Abner. It was all he could do at the moment. Whoever killed him had rudely shoved him through the passenger window, which opened to another passageway on the other side of the car. Abner's froggy, catatonic face blankly stared back. Reynolds tried fitting into the window but could barely get his shoulder in.

"Little buddy," Reynolds said. Genuine tears cascaded over him like the gasoline. He thought it was rain until he tasted the chemical burn on his lips and smelled the fumes.

Straddling the space between the cars above him was Kika. She was ghastly, covered in so much blood, she looked inhuman. She appeared to be floating, pouring industrial fuel from a large jerry can found by the immobilized backhoe.

Reynolds crossed himself.

Gasoline splashed her legs and boots as it poured down on him. When it emptied, she dropped the can on his head. Smiling but her teeth were black with blood.

"*Noooo!*" Reynolds struggled with his bulk.

Kika laughed. Blood bubbled at her neck wound, but she laughed. Her bloody tongue flickered obscenely. She gargled blood and spat on him.

The junkers trembled around him. Shank was hopping from one to the other.

Kika ignited the gold cigarette lighter that had belonged to Lady, which she'd taken from Abner. Fire bloomed on her hand and arm. She reached down with her blazing arm until flames coursed their way down to him.

His hair and face ignited and caramelized, then his chest, torso, and legs. Screams raw and guttural. He yelled for Abner, enflamed arms whipping back and forth.

Fire caught the hem of her dress, smoldering her legs. And it was fine. Flames licked and singed her as she vaulted the wall of crushed cars, and it was gratifying. It was a pleasure to burn, to be set aflame, to be conflagrant and demonic.

The fires she'd started were catching and spreading around the landfill. Several incendiary cauldrons bloomed. Slowly, all of it burned. But she wasn't fast enough to outrun the flames, and so, collapsed.

On the ground, she laid on her side, smoldering, sooty, and charred.

"Oh, glorious Hell!" Shank came up behind her, kicking dirt at Kika's smoking wounds. She dropped to her knees, patting her until the fire was snuffed. She scooped her up and carried her off, flames intensifying, licking close enough to singe. The shallow mote sent up a perimeter of fire. Kika had flooded the open graves with fuel and the fires grew to glorious heights.

They rendezvoused at Funzo's car. Fires were catching up, heat and fumes claiming their breaths and minds. Mari sat with her back to the car, coughing. She'd tossed the tattered bible and gun into one of the fires. Jubilee's head laid on her lap while Shank deposited Kika beside her.

Kika reached out for her sister, but Mari grabbed her wrist. "Jubi," Kika said.

"She's still breathing." Mari coughed. "Barely. If we don't leave now, we're going to die. I don't want to die."

Shank lifted them to their feet. She was the only one with enough strength to carry Jubilee in her arms. "Go through the smoke to the truck. Fast as you can!"

Running low to the ground, they moved around the fires, through smoke, to the truck. By the time they drove out the gate, there was nothing to look back on but dense, black smoke.

A light rain fell, increasing the smokiness, blackening the sky.

"When I get out of this town," Shank said, "I'm going on a mission to kill a lot more people for what they did to my family."

# CH. THIRTY-TWO

Silent surgery in a bathroom stall at a highway rest stop. Shank guarded the door. Kika sat quietly on the floor as Aries treated her. Dead quiet, but not dead. She looked ancient, her eyes dark and hollow after all the blood and soot washed off.

Aries carried a special clinical narcotics kit with him like a pro. Disinfectants, antibiotics, and painkillers helped to clean and bandage. They'd washed up as best they could in the sinks.

Aries sealed Kika's neck with duct tape after cleaning it. He mummified her burns with gauze and tape. Whatever painkillers he'd needled into her arm had completely anesthetized her.

Jubilee would need further hydration. Aside from a few cuts, scrapes, bruises, and mild burns, she was alive. The drugs had somehow preserved her. She was sleeping on a wooden bench against the tile wall, soiled hand-wipes at her feet. After she'd been cleaned up, she was given high dosages of monopotassium phosphate, along with water and soda. They'd changed her ragged clothes and put on fresh mechanic overalls bought at a gas station where they'd picked up other supplies.

Mari sat beside Jubilee, holding her hand. Fresh-bandaged face, arms, and legs, fresh clothes.

"Who knew you could buy T-shirts along with pork rinds and medical supplies at a gas stop?" Mari asked.

Back in the pickup truck, Shank turned on the radio to the hum of a mumbling preacher. She crossed herself, kissed her thumb. It was all she was ever going to listen to, going forward.

Five of them crowded the double cab. Broken glass glittered at their feet. The seats were streaked with Lady Hennessey's dried blood.

"Is Carbon burning?" Kika asked.

They turned to see the sky but were headed north by then.

# CH. THIRTY-THREE

"You said you'd never leave Carbon, and we did," Mari said. "Where are you taking her?"

"The fuck away," Kika said.

"We can go to Texas."

"Maybe."

Mari nodded. Sorrow chastened her words for the moment.

Shank drove the black pickup with a missing window and motorcycle secured in the back. Lady's body was also back there. There was a briefcase full of cash between seats.

Aries studied the three women from the passenger seat. Kika's eyes pierced back at him, her bandaged fists clenched and ready for another round. Jubilee was wide-eyed but withdrawn, awake but distant. Mari was the pulse between the three of them.

Aries bowed his head like a black, wooden Confucius, sitting there with jewels and knotty dreads coiled on top of his head. He looked them each in the face when he spoke. "We can only take you so far on this road. Shank and I gon' fight a big war. Even if you've helped us, we not the same tribe. Understand it's a family thing."

Kika agreed.

"Make sure you keep clean that wound on your neck," Aries told her. "There's potential for infection. Musta scared da bullet from ya bod 'cause I could not fin' it."

The truck cabin was hushed and motionless.

"Thank you," Mari said.

"Dying from gangrene would be the last laugh God has at my expense," Kika said. "Get us to Athens and I'll figure it out from there where we'll go."

"Your soul is ancient," Aries told her. "You've done this before. In another life, perhaps. An' maybe this your last time cyclin' 'round and you won' have ta repeat again. When next time you go, you go fa good."

Kika was granite. Unexpressive. Immovable.

"We got muthafuckas to address," Shank said. "We don' have dem guns, but we got God on our side."

Jubilee fell asleep against Kika's shoulder.

Mari held Jubilee's hand as they drove.

# CULMINACIÓN: HERMANAS CON CICRATICES

Change of faces, new locations. The trio often dressed in black, blending with the shadows. They were strangers where they went, traveling westward for several weeks. Hostels, hippie camps, cheap motels. Relying on quick and cheap cash labor. Sometimes petty crime and robbery. They roamed.

Mariposa's hair had grown past her shoulders, but if they ever settled down, she was going to shave her head bald.

Contracture scars mapped Kika's arms and face like tribal tattoos. She had shaved her head above her ears but left the top long. One half dyed crimson, the other deep black. Hiding behind a wide-brim hat that covered most of her face. Hiding the blistered skin that formed a tapestry of flames over her face, arms, and neck.

Jubilee's hair grew long. She'd suffered from aphasia, frequently mumbling nonsense that no one paid attention to. Sometimes she smiled. Mari was always at her side.

The three waited at a bus terminal connected to a diner. Dusk. Dim lights buzzed and blinked like the prostitutes that circled the parking lot. Several bums argued nearby. Somehow, the women fit into the scenario like the Wyrd Sisters.

"She'll get better," Mari said. "In time."

Still a specter in her long black coat and hat, Kika said, "This is just surviving."

"But she walks and sits when you tell her to," Mari said.

"Like a patient dog," said Kika.

"At least we'll give her a real home. Soon."

"You don't have to come along with us."

"Of course I do," Mari said. "Why wouldn't I? Aren't we safe now? Texas is a big enough place for us to disappear..."

The big, chrome bus hissed to a stop in front of them.

Kika grabbed Jubilee's hand and kissed her face, remembering photos of their childhood going up in flames, unsmiling little girls that curled up and turned to ashes.

**Thanks for reading!** Find more transgressive fiction (poems, novels, anthologies) at: Outcast-Press.com

Twitter & Instagram: @OutcastPress

Facebook.com/ThePoliticiansDaughter

GoFund.Me/074605e9 (Outcast-Press: Short Story Collection)

Amazon, Kindle, Target, Barnes & Nobel

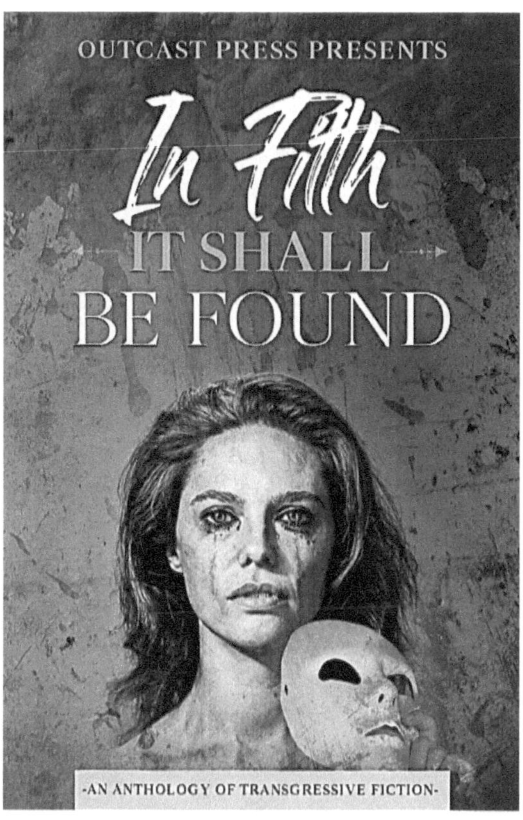


20 dark short stories by debut and veteran subversive writers like Craig Clevenger, Greg Levin, Lauren Sapala, Stephen J. Golds, and more! Everything from serial killers and speculative cannibals to strippers and smack addicts.

# MORE FROM OUTCAST PRESS

Henry Gallagher is going to die. His liver is failing and his chances of living past 30 crumble around him. He revels in a parade of violence, blackouts, half-hearted AA meetings, psych ward stints, dangerous sexual encounters, suicidal behavior, and shattered relationships. During his darkest hour, he receives an offer that threatens to change his life forever and a mental diagnosis that, in Henry's mind, makes him more monster than man.

# ABOUT THE AUTHOR

Twitter: @_MATorres_ and Instagram @_M.A.Torres

Originally from Brooklyn, New York, **Manny Torres** resides in Atlanta, Georgia. He is the author of the road-noir *Dead Dogs* and *Father Was a Rat King*. He's written and directed several documentaries and music videos, including *The Trespasser, Unendangered Species*, and *The Abby Go-Go Christmas Special.*

**Torres** is also a photographer and painter. For 15 years, he was a programmer and co-conspirator on *Step Outside: The Strange and Beautiful Music* program on WMNF 88.5FM in Florida. He is currently working on a series of crime novels.